THE VOICES WITHIN

SHORT STORY COLLECTION

THE VOICES WITHIN

SHORT STORY COLLECTION

JONATHAN MABERRY

CHRISTIE GOLDEN

DELILAH S. DAWSON

CATHERYNNE M. VALENTE

ANDREW ROBINSON

COURTNEY ALAMEDA

Published by Blizzard Entertainment.

Library of Congress Cataloging-in-Publication Data available.

ISBN: 978-1-956916-54-6

Manufactured in China

Print run 10 9 8 7 6 5 4 3 2 1

CONTENTS

TRIALS

JONATHAN MABERRY

The young orc moved like a shadow through the palm fronds.

The edge of the Northern Barrens was a beautiful place: countless trees heavy with fruit, the sound of songbirds calling above. The young orc had heard stories of how the night elf druid Naralex and others restored this once-arid land to the stunning glory that now lay before him. And yet there was great danger here, for all that rampant green majesty. There were scars upon the land if one knew how to look—old bones bleached white amid tangles of lush grass, broken blades, the rusted handles of war axes. The land remembered those who'd fought here. Those who'd bled and died here.

The orc expected it to feel like a graveyard—that was how his father had described it—but it did not carry that mournful melancholy. Instead, with each old weapon, each mark of fire on the oldest trees, he felt a sense of wonder.

I am walking through the history of my people, he mused. It was not the kind of thought he usually had. There was the weight of truth in it, as though he was on the verge of some greater understanding—as close to it as to the beast he now stalked. Something new trying to bloom in the soil of his soul.

He climbed atop a cracked boulder and squatted there, his hands automatically moving to touch his blades. Being alone out here was entirely different than he had expected. Long before he'd even left home for his first leg of the om'gora, he had been filled with excitement in all its many forms: The bravado that boiled in his chest when announcing to his parents he was ready. The thrill of the hunt. The delight in taking the first step toward acceptance. The hope of earning the next blessing after this one. But now those feelings had faded—not gone, but receded to a shadowy distance in his heart and mind. He'd felt the change happen slowly. The anticipation of the om'gora lasted still, but the fires beneath it had been banked. The fear was there, of course. He was young but not foolish.

Now what he felt, he was certain, was a sense of awe. Perched atop this boulder, hearing the wind rustling, the ferns pressing in on either side of him, staring down toward the gaping maw of the Wailing Caverns, he felt as if a thousand— no, ten thousand—orcs stood all around him. He was in their company, even if most were lost to time and battle. Some, he knew, had failed trying to complete this exact rite, here on this rock or within the thick darkness of the caverns.

He *felt* them.

He *was* them.

And on some level, he realized that this was likely his first real insight as an orc. Not as a warrior in training, but as one who might one day serve his people, should he live long enough to achieve that honor. Strange that even though he grasped his weapons, knowing a fight lay ahead that could only end in death, he could not feel any hate or bloodlust in his heart. He felt only peace. A kind of calm.

I accept death, he thought. Then he corrected that phrasing. *I accept that I can die.*

It was new to him, and he marveled at it, turning it over in his mind.

I might die today.

I might kill today.

We may both die—the beast and I—and that is okay. Natural.

These were not the thoughts of a youngling. They were edging very close to the musings of an orc grown. He smiled, and for a long moment he was pleased with it and with all it might mean.

And then from out of the mouth of the Wailing Caverns came a sound that swept all philosophy and introspection away. A roar. Deep. Hungry. Primal.

The youngling's mouth suddenly went dry as dust. His hands touched his weapons again, and now the youth—the boy—was back. And he was terrified, longing to be reunited with his armor. That feral, bestial cry came from the thing he had been hunting. A monster who had killed not just the many young orcs who had failed to best it during their own rites but also many battle-tested orcs and passing adventurers. The monster had littered the oasis with their bones and broken blades.

Trigore the Lasher.

The hydra bellowed out its cry to tell the upstart young orc that it *knew* he was there.

It was waiting for him.

And he was ready.

Ready to kill the beast and bring back proof to his people. To his family.

"I'm coming for you!" The young orc tried to summon all his courage and stand as tall and proud as an orc should. But his heart hammered in his chest, and the hands that gripped his axe and dagger were slick with sweat.

That feral, bestial cry came
from the thing he had been hunting.
A monster who had killed not just the
many young orcs who had failed to best
it during their own rites but also many
battle-tested orcs and passing adventurers.
The monster had littered the oasis
with their bones and
broken blades.

Still, he headed down the slope, desperate to ignore the claw marks raking through the dirt at the opening of the caverns. Being in motion seemed to help his faltering courage. Moving was itself an act of bravery. Of purpose. He began to grin as the first flickers of anticipation ignited in his chest.

"I'm coming for you," he said again, quietly this time. His pace quickened as he left the sunlit plains behind and allowed the darkness of the caverns to envelop him.

Before he could get his bearings, another blood-chilling roar ripped from the throat of the monster.

The glint of slitted eyes appeared, far, far above.

The hydra struck out with razor-sharp talons.

The orc dodged the attack and swung his axe.

"The death of that youngling marks another loss to the Horde," said Thrall as they left the council meeting at Grommash Hold. The council had been a grim one, where the main topic was the death of a young orc who had gone out on his om'gora but was clearly not yet ready. That morning a party of warriors had borne his body, torn and cold, back to the city.

Thrall and Aggra strolled down one of the many long dirt roads of Orgrimmar, heading in the direction of home, though neither was in any hurry to get there. Or anywhere. It was a fine afternoon, with a warm sun and a mild breeze stirring the leaves on the trees and the banners on the outer walls. Inside those defenses, shadows pooled between the homes and buildings, and the savory smells from scores of cooking fires wafted through open windows. And yet, for all that, their hearts were heavy.

"Another life taken by Trigore," mused Thrall darkly. "Why so many young orcs have chosen to try to track and kill that particular beast is a mystery to me. But I am heartened to know that the Horde will still rally to support the next attempts of our younglings."

Aggra gave a sad smile. "It will take a great orc to best such a beast." She paused. "Durak is becoming quite the young warrior, you know. You refused him last season, but he'll be ready soon."

Thrall did not meet her eyes. "I would never allow our son to track that monster."

"You think him weak?" Aggra asked sharply.

Thrall set his jaw in a hard line. "Weak? No. *Never.* But the om'gora is not to be undertaken lightly, as we have just seen."

"Durak is as strong as anyone of his age, *stronger* than most," insisted Aggra.

"Not arguing," Thrall assured her. In truth, he was shaken by the sight of the dead youngling. He looked around. "Speaking of Durak, where *is* our boy?"

"Rehze said he went fishing again," Aggra said. "He has a knack for coaxing the mackerel up to his line."

"We will eat well tonight." Thrall paused, then picked up the thread of their conversation. "It pains my heart to hear tales of our own taken by a rite meant to uplift our young."

Aggra laughed. "Says the wise and mighty orc who helped bring this practice into the ways of the Horde."

Thrall nodded. "While that is true, I don't have to like its every outcome." They walked a few paces before he sighed and added, "There are times I yearn for my early days as Warchief. No, don't look at me like that. I love what we have built here, and I would never want to go back. But it felt *different*."

"Or," said Aggra, "perhaps, wise as you are, you don't relate to what these younglings need to do in order to understand their strength and claim their power. After all, you were raised by humans; you did not complete such rites at that age. You had great battles to fight, a sea of injustices set before you. Your rites were in forging a better world, and in so doing, you have become who you are now."

He nodded again, taking her point. "Do I envy the opportunity these younglings have had since birth? Of course. Am I satisfied with how far our people have come? Yes. Especially after Garrosh, after Sylvanas—"

"So what troubles you now, am'osh?"

He glowered, but it crumbled into a rueful smile. "As a leader, a shaman, a father, I see this world is better. And yet . . . for all I've sought peace, sometimes I fear a world free from war. If Durak and Rehze come of age in a peaceful world . . . will they know why we fought? Have wisdom enough to recognize injustice, evil, cruelty when they see it? Possess the courage, the strength to face it? Even now I spend most of my time roaring and thundering in council meetings. I can hardly remember the last time I hefted a weapon."

He grunted as they passed a group of younglings dressed as self-styled heroes, wrapped in war cloaks made from tattered banners and helms of battered old cooking pots. They chased each other with swords and axes fashioned from dried palm fronds. While Durak was getting too old for those kinds of games, among them was their youngest, Rehze, who squealed as another young orc chased her, but then pivoted to deliver a clever backward slash that caught her pursuer across the stomach.

"That," he said, pointing. "That's what I really want to be doing."

"What? Making war again?"

There was a devious twinkle in his eye. "Of a kind."

With that, he threw back his head and uttered a war cry, snatched a branch free from a bush, and ran at the children, brandishing it like a weapon of legend. The younglings shrieked,

"As a leader, a shaman,
a father, I see this world is better.
And yet . . . for all I've sought peace,
sometimes I fear a world free from war.
If Durak and Rehze come of age in a
peaceful world . . . will they know why
we fought? Have wisdom enough to
recognize injustice, evil, cruelty when
they see it? Possess the courage,
the strength to face it?"

and Rehze, seeing her father, whirled and faced them all, holding her own mock weapon high.

"We are beset by an ogre!" she cried, rallying them—even the ones she was fighting a moment ago.

"Where is Durak?" growled Thrall. "What have you done with my firstborn, you monsters?"

Rehze stood firm in his path. "Durak is gagged and bound and is our rightful prisoner. You shall not find nor free him, for we sacrifice him tonight. He is ours by right of conquest."

Thrall loomed above them, menacing. "Free my son or feel my wrath."

"Feel *mine*!" Rehze bellowed. "Orcs of the Horde—to me!"

With her own battle cry, Rehze led the charge, meeting Thrall in the middle of the street. "Do you accept defeat? Do you submit?" she demanded.

Before he could reply, she leapt onto him and bore him backward, and then all the younglings were climbing over the great champion, toppling him, whacking him ferociously with their weapons.

Aggra stood there, laughing. She called out battle tactics, not to her partner, but to Rehze and her own little Horde.

Later, soundly defeated, Thrall sat on the edge of a stone well, tenderly probing all the sore places where little fists and feet, elbows and knees, sticks and clubs had landed their mark. Aggra sat beside him as Rehze ran off with the relentless energy of the young to start a new game that sent half the younglings running off while the others chased them.

"I'm getting too old for this," said Thrall, wincing at a particularly painful bruise on his ribs.

"You love it, and don't claim otherwise," countered Aggra, giving him a sharp but affectionate elbow to those same ribs.

"Rehze takes after you, that's for sure," he complained. "Lovely as a spring morning but fierce as a wolf with a bad tooth." He watched the game ebb and flow, losing track of the goals as the rules continued to change.

With a grunt for the effort, he and Aggra rose and headed down a side street where vendors had set up rows of stalls. There were weavers and metalsmiths, coopers and cartwrights, artists and the growers of every colorful fruit and aromatic herb. They browsed more than shopped, pausing now and then to talk to friends new and old. Many wanted to talk about the youngling who had died, and it was Aggra who engaged in those conversations, dissecting the situation, speculating on whether a party should be assembled to go after Trigore or if the glory should be left to a worthy challenger.

Thrall was content to listen. His heart was not drawn to such talk that day.

When her friends had dispersed, Aggra resumed the conversation. "You once told me how dearly Varok prized honor. What was it he said? *'Honor, young heroes . . . never forsake it.'*"

"Yes," said Thrall, surprised by the comment that seemed to come out of nowhere. "He was certainly right about that."

She studied his face. "Maybe that is what you yearn for, for our younglings. Honor. Something easy to claim in a just battle."

"Perhaps." He shook his head. "But with an equally high cost."

Aggra took his hand and led him out of the side street and onto a quiet lane beyond that wandered between a row of stables.

"War has cost me much," said Thrall. "Orgrim and Grommash. Cairne, Varok, Vol'jin—I often long for their guidance, friendship, understanding, but they are lost to me. Now I lead alongside their children, their successors, while I worry over how to prepare my own."

"All that they gave lives within you now."

"The memory of it, yes. But there are many times I wish the spirits I miss dearly would heed my call for counsel. Time has been generous—it has given me you, Durak, Rehze, the Horde—but it has also emptied the world of so many who deserved to live, to learn who they were beyond the field of battle. I feel robbed at times. Does that make sense?"

"Of course it does." Aggra was often fierce, even in her humor, though not at that moment. "But you are here now, thundering in your council meetings, shaping a new generation to battle with words and ideas, as well as axes and arrows. The Horde will grow stronger for your wisdom, and the wisdom of those who have made their mark on you. I know you will lead our people to greater heights, because I see how you have molded our young-lings. And that is also how I know Durak is ready for his om'gora."

Thrall leaned forward and touched his forehead to hers. A gentle act. She was surprised and resisted for a mere splinter of a moment, then she leaned into it. Sharing the moment.

His brow was swollen—a blow from Rehze's pointy little elbow—and Thrall winced, then laughed.

"Love hurts," said Aggra, then hugged him. "But its echoes are all around us. Our ancestors, our lost friends, they ripple through us, as our acts will ripple forward when we are gone. You are here, still. And for that, we are all glad."

They shared a smile before resuming their meandering walk through Orgrimmar.

"Honor includes caution," said Aggra. "I understand why you haven't pushed Durak to begin preparations for his om'gora, but you can't protect him forever."

"I know that," Thrall said, nostrils flaring. "But he is still young."

"But you are here now,
thundering in your council
meetings, shaping a new generation
to battle with words and ideas, as well
as axes and arrows. The Horde will
grow stronger for your wisdom, and
the wisdom of those who have
made their mark on you."

"There are those in this town who are younger than him but who've already taken the rites."

"And more than a few of them are dead," said Thrall. "The om'gora isn't to be undertaken for glory or to prove oneself. It is a pledge to serve, honor, and safeguard our people, and to know all that means. I know Durak is of age, but he is not ready. He *will* be, but for now he thinks it's all about being tough and brave, and that is such a small part of what he'll need to succeed."

Aggra gestured to some of the older children in the yard. "Some of his friends have already achieved their rites. That weighs on him."

"I know."

"And there are whispers of some doing so without their parents' blessings."

Thrall huffed. "I know that too. Which is why I'm glad Durak is wise enough to listen to us."

"So far," said Aggra. "A day may come when he will not wait. That reminds me," she added, "Rehze has been after you to explain the om'gora to her. She's jealous that Durak got the talk last winter."

Thrall nodded. "I shall take her for a walk when we get home. It's easier to speak away from everyone." He let out a belabored sigh. "Our young ones will learn the realities of our life soon enough. Battles and glory may make us strong, but we're stronger knowing why we fight. What we've lost and who we're fighting for." He paused for a long moment, then added, "It took me a long time to understand that and many other things Varok said."

"You didn't learn all of it from Varok." Aggra gave him a light jab. "Don't belittle my am'osh."

"Your am'osh has had more than his fair share of days of boneheaded bravado."

"Well . . . boneheaded . . . you're not wrong there . . . ," she conceded, and they both smiled.

Above them, the sun was a golden ball rolling slowly across the hard blue dome of the sky. There were a few puffy clouds sailing like a fleet of ships out on the far horizon. A flock of gulls coasted along on the air currents, angled so they seemed to hang unmoving in the sky. The giggles of the younglings filled their ears.

"At least our younglings are smart and brave," said Thrall. "And they both have heart and brains."

"They take after their mother in all the important ways," said Aggra airily.

"This I will not refute," said Thrall, and that was as far as he got because something small and very powerful came out of nowhere and raised her faux weapon to him.

"Show me your strength or die screaming, raptor dung!"

He looked down into the ferocious, glaring eyes of his youngest child. "I yield!"

"And so you should!" cried Rehze. "For I am a fierce warrior of the Horde!"

With that, she gave her father a crinkling smile, then put her fists on her hips, an unconscious imitation of her mother.

Thrall, grinning, stared at his wife and his daughter. They looked so alike and wore the same fierce, glowering looks. The same flashing eyes.

"Father, can you tell me of the om'gora? I want to learn *everything* about war and killing the enemy and hunting beasts and all of it."

Thrall shook his head. Then, off Aggra's head tilt, he conceded. "Yes. Let us walk."

"Walk where?"

"Anywhere. Just a walk so we can talk in private."

Rehze nodded vigorously.

"Let me say this first, Little Bug," he said. "The om'gora is not about war or killing. It is about learning what it means to be an orc. It's about learning how to be strong, yes, but also how to honor our ancestors, how to live in harmony with the elements."

Rehze stared up at him, half smiling as if he had made a joke, expecting a punch line after his words. Thrall caught Aggra's amused expression.

TRIALS

"I'll go start on dinner—I'm sure Durak will be home soon," said Aggra. "You two enjoy your walk. I think your father has a *lot* to tell you."

The creature's talons were little more than a moving shadow against the deeper blackness of the caverns. They came so fast that the young orc dodged almost too late. He threw himself down, rolled sideways, and sprang back to his feet, hoping for an advantage, but the darkness was so intense he saw nothing.

He circled, trying to find it. There was a movement, and once again it was black upon black, and he did not know if he was before or behind the monster.

Then it struck again.

This time, pain exploded across the orc's right side, and he staggered. But even as he lost balance, he saw a bit of its muscular shoulder, the curl of a wicked mouth, and the gleam of one merciless eye.

Terrified, the orc fought for balance and twisted, shuffling sideways to bring both his weapons up as he backed away toward the bright sunlight at the cavern's entrance. He swung a backhand blow with the axe and felt the blade strike something that yielded, but there was no death scream. The orc stumbled backward, and it followed him.

The creature was heavy, moving without hurry—either sure of its prey or cautious because of the blow it had just been dealt. Its breath came out as a ragged hissing, and the very ground seemed to tremble with its every step. The young orc smelled blood in the close air of the cavern. Some of it, he knew, was his own, but bigger than that, overpowering, was the stench of blood mixed with something like sulfur. Things crunched underfoot that were unmistakably bones.

"Come at me!" he said in a low growl.

Soon, the orc stepped backward out into the sunlight and settled into a fighting stance, knees bent for balance, weapons crossed before him, body crouched to avoid giving the beast an easy opening.

"Come *on*," he snarled.

It came.

One foot stepped gingerly out of the darkness, poised like one of the big hunting cats, though it was far larger. The creature stalked forward on two legs as big around as tree trunks, wrapped in scales that overlapped like plates of battle armor. There were countless scars on its legs from other young orcs who had failed to kill it during their rites.

The orc swallowed hard but did not retreat.

"Come on," he goaded. "Show your face . . ."

The hydra took another slow step, moving from utter darkness and into the glare of an unrelenting sun. Its claws gouged lines in the hardpan ground. And then it reared its heads.

All *three* of them.

The orc's blood turned to ice in his veins.

Three faces glowered down at him from atop long, muscular necks. Each was as hideous as the next, with crests of spikes rising from a reptilian pate. Scaly lips peeled back from rows of serrated teeth, the smallest of which was as long and sharp as the orc's dagger.

The young orc could actually *feel* the heat of its six eyes. Real heat, piercing and deadly. In the light of day, the orc could more clearly see that the creature's scaly body was crisscrossed with many scars drawn by sword and axe. Trigore the Lasher had fought many battles and had won them all.

Every single one.

The hydra took another step forward, and now he could see its tail—thick, long, and ending in a cluster of spikes like those on its head. It reared up on two massive legs and split the air with three dreadful shrieks.

It was at that moment that the young orc summoned his courage. This was what he had come all this way for—this battle. This fight. The om'gora demanded that an orc prove their

The om'gora demanded that
an orc prove their courage, but the
young orc felt his faltering. Still, he knew
he *had* to prove himself. Having set out on
this quest, it would be humiliating to return
in failure. That would cast a shadow over
his life forever. It would be better
not to return at all.

courage, but the young orc felt his faltering. Still, he knew he *had* to prove himself. Having set out on this quest, it would be humiliating to return in failure. That would cast a shadow over his life forever. It would be better not to return at all.

The realities of the moment cast their own shadow, though. He battled his own doubts and fears, while the creature was absolute in its own power and in the knowledge that it had survived *everyone* who had ever come hunting.

Every. Single. One.

All of this was a raging storm in the young orc's mind. With a cry of mingled fear and rage, he leapt forward, driving straight at the monster, feigning high with the dagger to distract and swinging his axe in a sidearm blow that was powered by all his muscle, every bit of his training, and every ounce of his bravery. The blade bit deep and blood exploded outward.

And it did him no damn good at all.

The next scream to fill the plains was his own.

Thrall and Rehze walked through the gates of Orgrimmar and left the city far behind.

It was cool in the shadows beneath the trees. An adder

slithered out of their way but stopped to watch them pass. Rehze smiled at it with an innocent joy that touched her father's heart.

"It's nice to have some time alone, Little Bug," said Thrall. "We don't get to talk much. You're either pestering Durak, hiding from your mother at chore times, or ambushing your poor old father."

"I beat you today!" she cried.

"You did," he agreed and tousled her hair. She swatted his hand away, giggling as she did so.

The arid land soon gave way to canyons made of red rocks that seemed to catch fire in the setting sun. With the haze rising in front of them, the crimson cliffs rippled and steamed. It was dryer out here than in the city, the heat less oppressive. Spiny lizards and dung beetles scuttled across rocks, and a seagull wheeled lazily far above it all.

They walked for nearly half an hour without saying much and instead seeing and hearing all that the natural world had to share. Thrall could feel his daughter growing calmer, losing that youthful agitation that always made her seem like there were ten of her. Now she strolled beside him with something akin to patience.

"Father . . . ?" she said after a while.

"Yes?"

"Will you tell me about the om'gora?"

"Yes. But why are you worrying over such a thing?"

She looked away for a moment. "I'm not *worrying*. I just want to know more about it. Harthog's older brother is planning on going out soon, even though that other orc just got killed. And it's all Durak's been talking about. I know what people say and all . . . but that's not the same as knowing what it means. It's not the same as knowing why we do it."

He glanced down at her. The request, though framed with a child's vocabulary, was a profound one. It was insightful, demonstrating depth of character.

"Tell me what you already know," he suggested.

She thought about that for a minute as they banked down a hill.

"I know there are three parts to it," she said.

"Three blessings, yes."

"One's about learning to respect the spirits of nature and the elements, and one's about honoring our ancestors."

"And the third?"

"Proving strength by hunting, I think."

Thrall nodded. "Yes to all three," he said. "And no."

"Huh?"

"Let's take them one by one. Let's start with the Blessing of the Land."

"I don't really know what that means," admitted Rehze as they passed beneath the little amount of shade provided by some palm trees here and there. "No one talks much about it. Or about the Blessing of the Ancestors. All the other younglings talk about is the rite to kill beasts."

"Not surprising. Hunting can be a lot of fun, and it builds character and skills. And the Blessing of the Clan has more exciting stories that get told more often. But between you and me, I think there's more to learn in the other blessings."

"What do you mean?"

He nodded his approval and sat down beside her. "The world in which we live is more than this," he said, gesturing to the sea, the fish, the arid land. "There are layers of reality everywhere, magic of many kinds. We who are called to be shaman naturally look deeper into the world."

Rehze's eyes widened in interest, urging him to go on.

He put a hand to her shoulder. "Close your eyes. Listen. *Feel.* What do you notice?"

They sat in silence for a time. He guided her fingers to the soil, digging her fingers in. There was a steady breeze that carried the sounds of wildlife to them, the scent of the earth. There was moisture in the deeper layers of the soil. The sun radiated heat down on them.

Rehze smiled. She was always one for finding beauty in the simplest things—from a squealing piglet to a fallen tree that housed a million insects, flourishing in the rotten timber. Thrall wondered, not for the first time, if she had a shaman's path in her future. Thrall looked around at the river and the sea, the hills and the arid landscape.

"The natural world blossoms where the elements meet. The elements find their own rhythm and harmony together. It isn't always calm, but even in turbulence they find balance." He paused, then, urging Rehze to open her eyes, continued, "But then we move in." He pointed to the city in the distance. "We need to hunt for food, cut down trees to build our homes, plant fields for crops. We *impose* ourselves on the land so that we can live, but if we take too much of it, we can throw the natural world out of balance.

"Every orc must understand that we live in harmony with nature and with the infinite elemental spirits that share this world with us. It is something to be joyful about, but it's also something that requires us to be vigilant and strong if we are to safeguard it. And it's the reason we honor the land through the om'gora."

Rehze gave that a lot of thought. They accidentally flushed a family of gulls from a nest in the tall grass and watched them fly away, scolding in their bird voices.

"I'm too small for the om'gora," she said. "Is there anything I can do *now*?"

"Little things," said Thrall. "But even little things add up over time. Picking up debris left by some careless other will matter. You can plant two new trees for each one our people cut down. You can take only what you need instead of treating resources as free and limitless. Do you understand?"

She nodded, her eyes wide and thoughtful again.

"In these acts, and others, we show our respect and gratitude to the land. This calls to the spirits of nature and brings them into our lives as welcome guests. During this part of the om'gora, the youngling goes to a shaman and asks that these spirits make themselves known, so that they might offer guidance to aid the land.

"A true shaman works in harmony with the spirits and the elements," he went on. "They might restore the presence of nature to a place sundered by battle or till manure into soil whose richness has been farmed out. These mundane tasks don't feel glorious, but they do great good. They nourish our world and our people. And done with an open heart, they cultivate humility. Do you know what that is?"

"Sure," said Rehze. "It means not thinking everything's just about you."

He gently tapped the top of her head. "You are a very, *very* clever bug."

"And what's the Blessing of the Ancestors about?" she asked.

Thrall mulled it over for a moment. "We orcs owe much to those who have come before us. If it was not for their courage, their vision, and their many sacrifices, we would not be the

"Every orc must understand
that we live in harmony with nature
and with the infinite elemental spirits
that share this world with us. It is something
to be joyful about, but it's also something
that requires us to be vigilant and strong
if we are to safeguard it. And it's
the reason we honor the land
through the om'gora."

people we are now. We would have no safe homes. We would be consumed by anger and the thirst for pain and blood." He shook his head. "Without understanding and honoring our ancestors, we could not truly value all that we have."

"Okay, but my friend Speartwig told me something about cooking. How does that honor the ancestors?"

Thrall smiled. "Some orcs have prepared a feast in honor of the ancestors, but there are other ways to honor their memory and their legacy. We might tell their stories, spread the lessons they learned far and wide for the betterment of all. We may right some wrong they did not have the opportunity to resolve in life, carry on their work. We can care for each other, as those gone once cared for us.

"Humility, kindness, benevolence, compassion . . ." he said. "These skills are more difficult to learn than swinging an axe, and yet they matter more to the longevity of our people. Even the sacred meals your Speartwig spoke of demand much— knowledge of herbs, when something is safe to eat according to the calendar of its growing. To orcs obsessed with combat, this may seem silly, and yet it is the heartbeat of our kind. It is what makes the Horde a community worth living in and fighting for."

Rehze bent to pick a flower and then stopped. She crouched down, looking at it instead.

"Tell me what you're thinking," coaxed Thrall.

"It's bruiseweed," she said slowly. Thrall waited. "If I pick it because it's pretty, it just dies, doesn't it?"

"Yes."

"But Mother says that bruiseweed is what some of the older folks take when their joints ache. Mother makes a paste out of it and puts it on cuts and scrapes. And sometimes she rubs it on me or Durak if we get a rash."

"All of this is true."

"I . . . can look at it and see how pretty it is," said Rehze, "but I don't *have* to pick it. Someone else might need it for medicine."

Thrall once more felt his heart lift.

She understands, he thought with great love and pride.

Rehze stood slowly and turned to look at him. He expected a smile but saw none. Instead, there was a faintness of unease in her eyes that he struggled to define. Was it because of all the weight and responsibilities of this long lesson?

"Tell me about the other rite. That's the hunting one."

"The Blessing of the Clan," he supplied. "Come, let's sit beneath the palms and watch the water. There are these little fishes that sleep in the dried mud for months and then wake up when it rains. We'll see if we find any."

They sat and watched the waters of a small river ambling toward the sea, sunlight sparkling on the tiny wavelets.

"We orcs need to be strong, and we need to be tough. Able to fight, to hunt, to protect our families. But that isn't the reason for that rite of om'gora. It just *looks* like it from a distance." Thrall pointed down to the stream. "Tell me what you see."

She leaned forward, elbows on her knees, and really looked. "I see . . . pebbles. There's a blue one and some green ones."

"What else?"

"I see an old buckle someone must have lost."

"And . . . ?"

"Ooooh!" she cried with sudden delight. "There's a fish! It's purple with a pink tummy!"

"Perfect. Now, if you just walked past the stream and looked quickly, then all you would have seen is the water. But when you observe with patience, you see so much more." He looked at her. "Do you understand the lesson in that?"

Rehze thought about it, still watching the water, then she nodded. "I think so."

"Then how might that apply to the Blessing of the Clan?"

She hmmed at that, and it delighted Thrall that it was clear she *was* thinking it through. "You're saying that I only know about om'gora from a distance. I'm hearing about it—looking at it—but I'm not *seeing* it?"

Thrall smiled and gestured toward the north. "From a distance, the Horde looks like warriors, fighters, killers. We prize strength of arms, hold passion for combat, but only someone looking and not seeing would think that it is because we treasure war."

"But we *do* treasure war. It's how the Horde has won all its battles, isn't it?"

Thrall smiled grimly at that. "The Horde has won many battles and lost many too. Not all of them on the field of war," said Thrall, patient. "The strength we orcs acquire by hard training, by dangerous rites like the Blessing of the Clan, through warfare with enemies who must be fought, is not what defines us. It is not the bloodshed that we seek anymore."

"Then I don't understand."

Thrall nodded. "We have how many pigs in our yard?"

"Huh? Pigs? Oh . . . seventeen. And Old Vhreega is about to drop a litter."

"Correct. And we raise pigs for food, yes?"

"Yes . . . ," she said cautiously. Rehze was not at all a fan of killing any of the family's livestock and sometimes wept bitterly when a pig was slaughtered.

"You know that we must do this or else we will go hungry. Sure, we can eat vegetables and grains, but we eat meat too. That means that we have to kill the animals we raise."

"I hate that."

"I know," said Thrall kindly, "but you eat your meat all the same."

She said nothing.

"From a distance, the Horde
looks like warriors, fighters, killers.
We prize strength of arms, hold passion
for combat, but only someone looking
and not seeing would think that it is
because we treasure war."

"When your mother or Durak or I kill an animal, do you think we do it out of hatred?"

"No . . ."

"Does it mean we think nothing for those animals?"

"No, but . . . I . . . guess we have to."

"Why?"

"Like you said, we have to eat."

"Exactly," said Thrall. "Violence is sometimes necessary. We kill livestock for food. We fish the waters for food. We hunt the lands for food. Have you ever heard an orc curse at any animal that's being killed for these reasons?"

Rehze shook her head. "Of course not. But all the fighters in the city talk of killing enemies. They even sing songs about it."

She spoke true of a long tradition among the orcs: lok'tra, songs that told the glories of battle and of great wars dating back through time. Rehze knew the lyrics to many of them and often sang these war songs when she played. Durak, on the other hand, favored lok'vadnod—songs of orc heroes. The difference mattered, as Thrall saw it. His son was on the edge of adulthood and that was a personal thing, as heroism is personal. Whereas for Rehze such things were really an abstraction, and at her age it was easier to play at war than want to be a hero.

"Sure," he said, "but we do not sing to idolize violence. We sing to carry forward the memory of injustice, to honor those brave enough to meet it with steel. I pray you won't live to see such evil, but the songs of our people may grant you the wisdom to know what to do if you must face it."

At this, she beamed. "Strike it down!"

"Exactly," he said again. "Now listen, it is important for younglings to undertake a quest for the Blessing of the Clan, and more importantly to do it without friends or family watching. No one to cheer them on. No one to come and save them. They must learn how strong they are. It is a very important truth that the Horde is only as strong as those who serve it. In war, one poor soldier can cause a line of battle to falter. A weak link can break the strongest chain."

She nodded, engrossed by what he was saying. Thrall wanted to hug her close, to tell her to stop growing so that he might protect her always. But he knew too well the importance of the lesson, a lesson his own parents had not lived long enough to impart to him.

"The Blessing of the Clan is no easy thing for a youngling. It's frightening to be alone and to know that their survival depends solely on what they do. They might find themselves moving through unknown terrain, seeking resources like food, water, and shelter while spending days tracking the beast. This requires intelligent observation and equally intelligent decision-making. And when the beast is confronted, they have to fight and kill it.

TRIALS

This proves they can do that—that they can overcome something bigger, stronger, possibly wiser, certainly more experienced, and many times more dangerous. So much is learned by that."

Rehze shuddered, looking askance. "Some get killed. Some orcs, I mean. Like . . ." She trailed off rather than name the orc lad who lay dead back in the city. Thrall understood the hesitation some—especially the very young—had for naming the dead aloud.

Thrall thought of that morning's council meeting. "Yes," he said, "some die, and that is a sad and terrible thing. It's a loss to their families and to the entire Horde. We all grieve. But at the same time, we learn from what happened. Did the orc go out too soon? Were they properly trained? Had they not only heard the advice of their elders but *heeded* it, understood it? And those who knew someone who died, gain deeper—although painful—knowledge of how the loss of a single family member can weaken our people."

"Then why risk it at all?"

"You tell me."

She took a long time sorting through that one. Again, Thrall did not interrupt. In a way, this was practice for her own om'gora, because he was letting her discover her own insights. Parenting, he mused privately, was as difficult and demanding as being a warrior. Maybe more so.

Rehze finally summoned the words she sought. "Because . . . the next orc who goes out will maybe wait until they're older," she said cautiously. Thrall nodded in approval and twirled a thick finger to encourage her to go deeper. "And . . . because they know that risking their life risks the Horde too."

"Indeed. They lost the orc and all that orc could have *been*," agreed Thrall. "All that orc might have *become*."

Rehze looked at him and then away. "You were a slave," she said in a very small voice. "You were there when the orcs were prisoners and kept in camps. But you overcame that. You fought for yourself and everyone else. I wouldn't even be here. Or Durak. Or . . . maybe the whole Horde. You saved everyone a bunch of times. But if you had died a youngling . . ."

It was a shockingly wise insight for a child, and Thrall could hear the clear echo of Aggra's wisdom in Rehze. That made his heart swell with pride, and with love.

"It has been my honor to serve our people, in war and in peace," he said.

Rehze stood straight, a twinkle of mischief in her eye. Suddenly the maturity was gone from her face as she adopted a haughty, regal expression. "And now you will serve *me*. Kneel!"

Thrall immediately dropped to one knee and bowed his head, spreading his arms wide in supplication. "I bow to Warchief Amarehz, Chieftain of the Orcs of Azeroth, benevolent

"You were a slave,"
she said in a very small voice.
"You were there when the orcs were
prisoners and kept in camps. But you
overcame that. You fought for yourself
and everyone else. I wouldn't even be
here. Or Durak. Or . . . maybe the whole
Horde. You saved everyone a bunch
of times. But if you had died
a youngling . . ."

mistress of all she surveys, mistress of beasts and birds and all things that walk, fly, wriggle, climb, crawl, and wallow. Overlord of Quilbeasts, Squisher of Toads, Tamer of Zhevra, Tickler of Wolves, Official Despiser of Hog Stew, Grand Deflater of Swellfish, and Midnight Procurer of Biscuits from the Secret Stash of the Farseer Aggralan the Almighty. To you I bow in humility and deference."

Rehze tried to maintain her imperial haughtiness, but the silliness snuck past her resolve and she collapsed into laughter. Thrall caught her and they tumbled to the grass together.

They stopped laughing to gaze up, and Thrall held her close. Clouds tumbled across the sky above them, each one looking like some rare animal. For a few minutes—when their laughter had finally dwindled—they began pointing to one or another, calling out what they looked like. Most of Thrall's observations were for rare animals, while Rehze pointed to a very fat one and said that it looked like her father after a feast.

Thrall considered for a moment, lips pursed, and Rehze paused, as if she had gone too far. But Thrall said, "I can see it."

They laughed again, but it didn't last long as the fingers of twilight pulled the sun toward the west.

"Father?" said Rehze, her tone growing serious again. "What we were talking about, you being a slave, having no family growing up . . . no good times like we have. And now having to be a shaman and representative and everything else for our people . . ."

"What about it?"

She sat up and stared at him with huge eyes. "That . . . that's a lot to carry."

He got to his feet and pulled her up too.

"Yes," conceded Thrall. "But every orc of the Horde needs to be able to carry the burden of protecting our people and providing for them. That is why the om'gora exists, to show that the strength of our people can't be measured by having killed or even having won a battle. Our people's strength is built on *more*."

"Is that why you told Durak that he wasn't ready yet?" asked Rehze flatly. "Because he thinks it *is* about being tough and being able to kill monsters?"

"Yes. He wasn't happy about it, and I don't think he's ready to understand something so important. That's why your mother and I suggested he wait. But he's a good son, and he has something greater than courage. He has heart. That will count for much when his time *does* come."

"Yes . . . ," she said and then looked away.

He saw a shadow cross Rehze's face, and she turned farther away. When she did not turn around, Thrall asked, "What is it? What is stealing your joy?"

Rehze spoke in a small and fragile voice. "Truth."

It was said with heavy emotion that Thrall tried to understand. Worry, for sure, but also sadness, regret, and . . . was it shame?

"Little Bug," he said, "you must tell me what's wrong. You were full of glee one moment and now you look wretched."

"I made a promise not to tell," she said.

"If it is a promise that will do no harm, then keep it," said Thrall after a moment's consideration. "But if that promise is a dangerous one, then tell me."

Without turning, she said, "The orc who died. Benge. I saw him when they brought him in. He was all cut up. His . . . father turned away from him, but I don't know if it was because of how bad he looked or because . . . because he failed to kill the thing that did that to him."

"Of course Benge failed. He went after *Trigore the Lasher*, and it is too fierce for so young an orc to face. Trigore has killed many grown orcs and Horde warriors, Alliance too. No one blames the boy for failing. Not even his father. More likely his father was grieving because his son may have gone out too soon. Many of us parents share that fear. After all, how can we ever know if sending our younglings out for these rites will help them grow . . . or end their lives?"

A sob broke in Rehze's chest, and her body began to tremble. Thrall took her by the shoulders and gently turned her around.

"Amarehz," he said now, invoking her full name. "What is it? You must tell me."

"It's . . . it's Durak."

"What about him? Are you worried that he will face Trigore next year when he goes out for his om'gora? I won't permit it, and—"

"But, Father, Durak *has* gone out."

Thrall froze all the way to his marrow.

"What?" he demanded.

"That's why he's not around today. Benge was his friend, and Durak was so mad that Trigore killed him. He went out just after dawn to hunt the hydra and kill it himself. For Benge . . . and to prove he is ready for his rites."

"No," breathed Thrall as the icy terror gripped him. "No, no, no." Even as he spoke, he rose up, grabbed Rehze, and began running back toward the city.

The journey to the Wailing Caverns was far, but they were upon Moonpaw, and the great wolf seldom tired during times of great exertion. Three of Thrall's most trusted orc warriors rode with them, and Aggra galloped beside Moonpaw on another huge borrowed wolf.

JONATHAN MABERRY

Even so, the sun was edging toward the horizon and threw long shadows behind it.

"Will he be okay?" cried Rehze.

But Thrall, fearing what words of panic and terror would escape him, said nothing. There was a pain in his chest that felt like an arrow had been shot through his heart.

They passed through Durotar and into the Northern Barrens. They sped past the crossroads and rode hard for the large brown mountain beyond it, pressing on, taking shortcut paths they knew, racing against the setting sun. It seemed to take forever, but then the gray walls of the Wailing Caverns rose out of the twilit gloom.

From far away, they saw someone sprawled in the dirt, sitting with their back against a boulder, legs splayed, arms slack. The dying sunlight painted the figure, and Thrall feared that the bloody red he saw was not *all* from the sun. He had been on enough battlefields to know a grave wound from any distance.

"Durak!" cried Rehze, and both father and daughter leaped from Moonpaw's back and raced like the wind down the slope to the mouth of the caverns, Aggra close on their heels.

As they drew near, their hearts began to break, for the figure was indeed covered with gore. The orc warriors fanned out, blades drawn, eyes fierce and blazing. Thrall, Aggra, and Rehze cried out in horror as they saw that the shape before them was indeed Durak. But soon the image of death and destruction seemed to undergo a strange process of change. At fifty yards they were looking at the corpse of Durak, smeared with his own lifeblood. But at fifteen yards, a new truth emerged.

Durak sat on the ground with his back to the rock. His clothes were slashed and torn, and he bled from a score of cuts, some deep and terrible. His face was painted with blood. Yet it was not the dark red—nearly black—blood of an orc. No, this was something much brighter.

It was truly *painted*. The marks were crooked and sloppy, but there was an order to them, a pattern. The bright red blood on his face matched the dark red on the fingers of his hands, and that ignited the smallest spark of hope. One bloody hand gripped the edge of the rock, and with a great effort of will, Durak rose to his feet. He stood there, bloody, swaying, but *alive!*

Thrall reached out to him first, but Durak did not embrace him. As if performing a conjurer's trick, the young orc instead reached down behind the rock and lifted something. It was a horrifying, dreadful thing to see, and yet it filled Thrall's heart with joy.

It was one of the severed heads of a hydra, that most dread beast—Trigore the Lasher.

"My boy," cried Thrall. "What have you done?"

Durak looked at his father and mother. "So, *now* will you let me do the om'gora?"

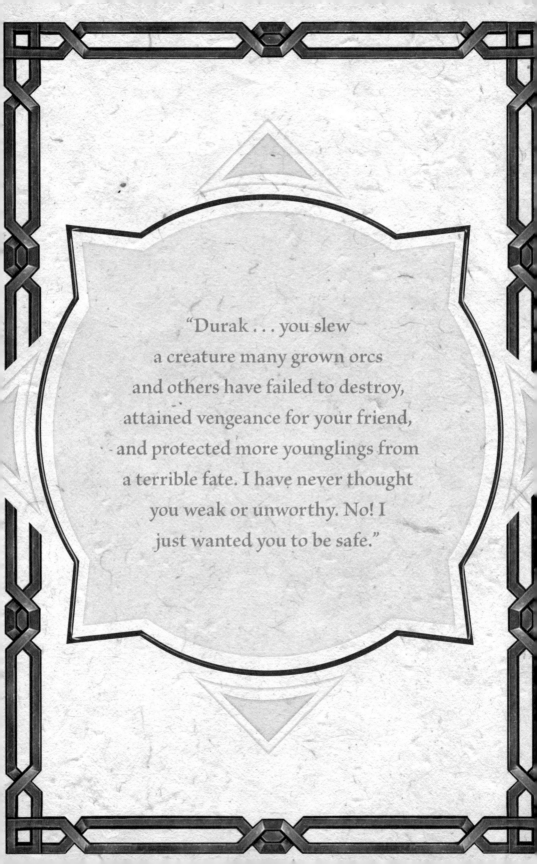

"Durak . . . you slew
a creature many grown orcs
and others have failed to destroy,
attained vengeance for your friend,
and protected more younglings from
a terrible fate. I have never thought
you weak or unworthy. No! I
just wanted you to be safe."

TRIALS

Durak gestured weakly with his other hand, and behind him, barely visible in the shadows of the cavern's mouth, were two more huge lumps of flesh, gristle, and spikes. Sightless green eyes staring up at the sky.

"I . . . I wanted to show you," wheezed Durak. "Father, I wanted to . . . show you that . . . I'm ready—"

Thrall took Durak gently into his powerful embrace and pressed his forehead to his son's. Aggra leaned in to join them. Rehze took one of Durak's hands and held it tightly, pressing it to her chest.

"My son," Thrall finally said, his voice filled with wonder, with pride and love. "Do you know what you've done?"

"I . . . killed the monster, Father," whispered the boy. "I . . . wanted to make you proud, to show you that I can serve our people with honor. You said I wasn't ready for my om'gora . . . but I wanted to . . . show you . . . that I am."

"Durak . . . you slew a creature many grown orcs and others have failed to destroy, attained vengeance for your friend, and protected more younglings from a terrible fate. I have never thought you weak or unworthy. No! I just wanted you to be safe. And . . . and . . ."

Thrall was unable to finish. He was laughing too hard, and weeping.

They sat around a campfire that blazed so brightly it filled the whole plain with a warm, golden light. Even the mouth of the cavern looked less grim, almost cheerful.

After Thrall and Aggra dressed Durak's wounds, he needed to rest. Aggra had sent Rehze running into the fields to gather certain revitalizing herbs. They worked together, changing bandages and fetching water.

He sat close to Durak.

"You slew Trigore the Lasher," he said. It was perhaps the twentieth time he'd said it. Each time he laughed and shook his head. "You're as mad as the moons, but no one will ever question your courage."

"I might test that courage by hitting you upside the head with an axe handle," muttered Aggra as she began dressing another wound. "Knock some common sense into you." Then, as if she heard the bitterness in her own voice, Aggra snorted, grinned, and jerked the ends of the bandage tight.

Durak gasped in pain.

"Brave young orc complaining of a scratch," she said.

Rehze chuckled under her breath.

Durak licked his dry, cracked lips. "So, will . . . will you let me do the rest of my om'gora?"

"Well," said Thrall, feigning doubt, "having tasted your cooking on hunting trips, I think you preparing a meal to honor the ancestors might classify as an act of war."

Rehze tried not to laugh out loud but snorted instead.

Moonpaw lumbered over and sniffed the hydra blood on Durak's clothing, uttering a low growl.

Durak glowered at the wolf. "Does everyone in this family have an opinion?"

Thrall sighed. "Your mother and I will discuss your om'gora, and this time, you will wait for us before charging ahead." He nudged his son's shoulder.

Durak smiled through his bandages as the cinders of the family's fire rose into the night sky, carried across the Northern Barrens by the wind.

THE
CALLING

CHRISTIE GOLDEN

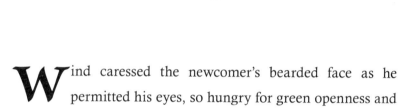

Wind caressed the newcomer's bearded face as he permitted his eyes, so hungry for green openness and soft lands, to feast.

Stormsong Valley was the ancient home of the tidesages, mages whose mastery of water and wind had protected ships and sailors for generations. Yet the beauty of this little hamlet near the sparkling sea was not that of majestic monuments to powerful magic. Here, it was obvious one was in the breadbox of Kul Tiras, where a salt-spray wind whispered over barley and wheat and the only magic was that of water and windmills, creaking from morn till night, transmuting elements to energy in service of the feeding and care of ordinary folk.

The pleasant sound of the mills sang a promise of new beginnings.

And the crash of the waves below, near the cave where his belongings lay bundled and buried, spoke of an ending.

Anduin Wrynn's recent wandering had not taken him to peaceful places. He understood that he was trying to scour himself, to purge his mind and soul, to burn away his sins in places where the landscape reflected his own suffering.

My friends . . . the ones I almost killed. They believe my hands are clean. But they don't feel clean.

Years after that confession, they still didn't.

Hands that had once warmed with the Holy Light. Healed body and spirit. Protected a kingdom, a world.

He flexed them now; he and his hands were anxious to keep busy.

As a boy, Anduin had yearned to travel Azeroth, seizing what chances he could—manufacturing them sometimes—in search of adventure. Now, he sought to escape, not explore. Adrift, alone, he turned his hand to whatever would earn him that day's meal and a place to sleep, even if sleep was a capricious comfort. Slumber sent night terrors from which Anduin would awaken screaming as often as not, rather than gifting him true rest, or even simple oblivion.

In a way, his waking mind was a better friend. There were many places Anduin knew his feet had trod, but he had only fragments of memories of them. Sometimes his mind restored

As a boy, Anduin
had yearned to travel
Azeroth, seizing what chances
he could—manufacturing them
sometimes—in search of
adventure. Now, he sought
to escape, not explore.

them to him, in the form of moments where he seemed to relive the very thing he did not wish to remember, the recollection more horrifying than the original wound.

Changing his environment helped, as did learning something new. Keeping his hands busy, playing a game of hide-and-seek with personal demons much worse than true ones. Then on to the next place, and the next.

Anduin had kept to himself on the voyage to Kul Tiras, as he always did. He stayed in his cabin, venturing topside only when the walls of the cabin closed in and the air stank of his own fear and sour sweat. He silently observed the sailors making knots, then fashioned his own—a skill he would take from the trip. Once the ship had docked, Anduin slipped into a dark corner of a tavern and ordered a bowl of stew.

He was not among those who sought solace at the bottom of a tankard. He acknowledged there was some temptation in the thought of drinking deeply enough to drown the dreams of his body moving against his wishes, of watching his hands curl around the hilt of his father's corrupted blade. But he knew the only thing worse than living with those memories would be losing control.

Anduin ate the meal without tasting it, listening to news, gossip, and who needed what done where, and he learned that Stormsong Valley was flourishing so well that there was a lack of strong backs willing to help with harvests, tend the land, or grind the grain.

The long walk from Boralus to the valley had calmed him, each step bearing him from the bustle of the harbor into silence, stillness, and the steady rhythm of the sea.

"That's my favorite view," came a voice from behind.

Anduin whirled, reaching for the sword that was not there, the sword that was safely hidden in a cave below his feet. The sword that hung over head and heart. Seeing his startlement, the approaching figure, a man of middle years, held up a hand and smiled reassuringly. He had bright blue eyes, and what little hair he had left was nearly all gray.

"My apologies. Seems even with this leg, I can still move quietly." He gestured, and Anduin could see by the way the man hobbled, leaning on a staff for aid, that the leg had once been badly broken and had not mended fully.

I could help, he thought, then remembered that time was over.

The man continued. "I proposed to my wife here. Saw my last sunset before I left for the Fourth War, and the first when I made it home. When you've seen what I've seen . . ." He sighed and fell silent. Anduin was glad the stranger did not finish his sentence. "Well, the heart longs for quiet. Simple beauty. Things that grow and change, and things that don't. I'm Rodrik Feldon, by the by."

"Jerek." Anduin had used the alias before, starting in simpler times as a youth running from responsibility. He was running from much darker things now. "I'm looking for work."

"I'm looking for help. What's your calling, Jerek?" The casual question was unexpected, and for a moment, Anduin couldn't breathe.

A calling.

He thought of the priesthood and of Aerin Stonehand, the young Ironforge warrior assigned to train him in the art of the sword. She had promised to "dwarf-temper" him, but instead realized the prince was not suited to cause pain. To harm. Aerin believed that Anduin might thrive in service to the Light. So had Magni Bronzebeard.

Anduin had believed it too, once. He'd always felt drawn to the peace it offered. The stillness.

My whole life, I've wanted peace, he thought. *And my whole life, I've never had it.*

Fields by the ocean. Open sky, open land. Hard physical labor. Maybe this place, this job, would help.

Light knew, nothing else had.

Anduin realized his mind had wandered and Rodrik was waiting for his answer. "I'm a jack-of-all-trades," he said. Off Rodrik's bemused gaze, he added, "I learn fast, my back's strong, and I'll work hard."

Rodrik took in Anduin's tattered cloak and mud-spattered boots, his unkempt beard and dirty hair. "You look like you've come a long way, son. Where have you traveled from?"

Anduin bristled, alert. "Does it matter?"

Rodrik fixed him with a long, appraising gaze. "You seem a bit on edge," he remarked. "And hungry. Here. This might help." He reached into his pack and procured a loaf of bread.

Anduin took it. The loaf was still warm, and the smell made his stomach rumble. Rodrik nodded toward the windmills dotting the landscape. Their arms turned and creaked, but there was a lone water mill some distance away. A channel diverted the river's stream toward a huge wheel. Bags of wheat and barley were piled high beside it, waiting to be milled, and chickens pecked industriously at stray grains. A short walk away was a small, cheerful-looking cottage, where a horse, a goat, and her kid cropped in the nearby grass.

"The water mill's mine. You'll have plenty of bread and goat's milk. Eggs too, if you keep the fox away. I'll work you hard, which you say you want, and pay you fairly. You'll need training, of course, but if you're a quick learner, it won't take long. After that, I'll be by once or twice a week with supplies."

Rodrik went over Anduin's list of responsibilities: checking the millstones, grinding the grains to flour, maintaining the machinery, taking orders—

"Wait," Anduin interrupted. His throat tightened; he hadn't thought this through. "The farmers will bring the grain *here*? How many? How often?"

He could hear his voice rising with agitation and feel his palms starting to sweat. He had sought isolation, but this sounded like it would provide exactly the opposite. Anduin felt himself shutting down, as if, one by one, doors inside him were closing. This place, pleasant as it seemed, didn't have the answer after all.

"Oh, I used to be interrupted all the time, but I moved my family into town after the war. My wife runs a bakery now. I do all the boring work, and I'll handle the orders. I turned over the hard part to the young and strong." Rodrik chuckled ruefully. "It was a good idea in theory, but I can't keep anyone for long. It gets too lonely, or so I hear—"

"I'll take it."

As Rodrik had warned, there was training—quite a lot of it. The older man taught him how to "listen" to the mill to know when something was off and how to repair the intricate machinery. How to test the grind of the flour by the miller's "rule of thumb"—its feel between thumb and forefinger—and how to inspect the grindstones themselves. How to milk the goat, saddle the horse, and make a snare to catch the fox if it bothered the chickens.

Anduin paid keen attention. The sooner Rodrik deemed his new hand ready, the sooner Anduin would have his privacy. He was silent except to ask or answer questions, but Rodrik didn't seem to mind. He chatted amiably, mostly about his family: his wife, Vera, who not only managed the bakery but was also the baker herself; their son, Ben, a decade younger than Anduin; and their daughter, Cynda.

"She's still a child yet, but smarter'n most adults I know. Gets that from her mother." And her father smiled, his eyes full of pride.

Anduin stayed silent. His own family had been nothing like Rodrik's. His mother had died shortly after he was born, lost to violence; his father had been hurting, distant, and for many years, gone. When Rodrik spoke of his service in the Fourth War, Anduin withdrew even further.

"There weren't an awful lot of professional soldiers in Kul Tiras right before the war began," Rodrik said as Anduin sifted various grinds of flour through his fingers. "The majority were drafted, and most from around here weren't all that familiar with the weapons of war. We're farmers, millers, beekeepers. You should have seen me the first time I held a sword!" He

Bodies, wrapped in white,
laid out on the weathered boards
of the harbor. A pitiful few soldiers
in armor waiting to board . . . and
Genn's words: "That's the last of
the soldiers. We'll be calling
up farmers next."

chuckled, then grew serious, his eyes somber. "I learned how to use it pretty well, though."

Anduin's breath caught and his heart hammered.

Bodies, wrapped in white, laid out on the weathered boards of the harbor. A pitiful few soldiers in armor waiting to board . . . and Genn's words: "That's the last of the soldiers. We'll be calling up farmers next."

"Jerek?"

"S-sorry," Anduin stammered, staring at his hand, clenched tightly around a fistful of flour. He let it fall and, muttering an excuse, strode quickly out of the millhouse, his lungs suddenly tight and hungry for air.

Once his training was complete, Anduin's days were filled with the simplicity of hoisting sacks and pouring grain into the hopper, bagging flour, maintaining the equipment, and tending the animals. Through every hour ran the rhythmic, soothing splash of the waterwheel.

The only thing on Rodrik's list that Anduin had neglected to accomplish was the snare for the fox. Thus far, it had left the chickens alone, and Anduin disliked the idea of killing the creature at all, let alone for something it *might* do. He was also aware that he couldn't keep an eye on the birds all the time, and foxes were sometimes active during daylight hours.

At first, Anduin had only heard its sharp yips and barks at twilight. Then, on the nights he stayed out to stargaze, Anduin often caught sight of a shadowy shape just beyond the ring of firelight and a pair of glowing eyes analyzing him with no hint of fear. One night, on impulse, Anduin sliced off a piece of meat from the roasting stick.

"Hey. Fox," he said, and tossed it to the creature. It danced out of the way, confused, but quickly realized its error. It gulped down the morsel, then darted off.

It returned the following night, though, sitting gracefully with its forepaws together and its bushy tail curled around them, as if it were properly introducing itself to him.

"I shouldn't feed you, fox," Anduin said. Its ears flicked as it listened. Strange, to hear his own voice. He had said as few words to Rodrik as possible and stayed silent otherwise.

A pink tongue crept out to lick a smudgy black muzzle.

I really shouldn't feed you, Anduin thought, but he did, and wondered why.

His nightmares had eased, ever so slightly, with this regimen of physical labor, solitude, and simple tasks, but they had not disappeared. Nor had shame, or the gulf of regret and remorse. Often, he felt an invisible weight as heavy as the millstone, and

His nightmares had eased,
ever so slightly, with this regimen
of physical labor, solitude, and simple
tasks, but they had not disappeared.
Nor had shame, or the gulf of regret
and remorse. Often, he felt an invisible
weight as heavy as the millstone, and
equally capable of crushing him.

equally capable of crushing him. No, it was best to just take things day by day, hour by hour. Task by task.

Keeping his hands busy.

Anduin looked forward to the nights when he was too tired to dream. The content of the dreams varied, but the one constant thread was violence. *His* violence. Anduin was as helpless in these dreams as he'd been when he'd performed the brutal acts. Sometimes the dreams took the form of flashbacks, paralyzing him in a dreadful state between past and present.

The dreams were terrifying when they devastated him and racked him with guilt.

They were worse when they didn't.

Thunk.

The axe bit deep into the wood, splitting it cleanly as Anduin's body moved in a practiced rhythm. Strike. Reset. Strike. Reset. New log.

Thunk.

Strike.

Small forms, gossamer wings, so fragile, the wide eyes, wider in terror—

Reset.

THE CALLING

Thunk.

The sword, so like the one in his father's fist, but twisted, blasphemed, glowing not red, not golden, but blue—pretty, almost, wasn't it? Plunging in, the serrated blade piercing, then sawing as it was withdrawn, the wide eyes blank, and the scream, *musical, abominable, the* scream—

Anduin staggered back, his throat raw, his mouth open and gasping for breath. The log at his feet was not simply split, but reduced to tiny slivers of kindling. His hand still gripped the handle, aching, the knuckles white, and he threw the axe as if it had burned him. It landed harmlessly in the dirt, but Anduin had not even looked before he had thrown it.

His legs felt weak, and he sank down, placing both trembling hands on the good, rich soil. He couldn't be trusted. He didn't even know when he was going to lose control.

The thoughts, like predators sensing weakness, pressed into his mind. *What if I call the Light and it doesn't answer?* He'd felt no brush, no hint of it. Even the ache in his Light-mended bones had vanished, and with it any hope of guidance.

Which of us—the Jailer, the soul within the shard, me—felt that awful thrill of exhilaration?

What if I take a life and I feel pleasure?

Anduin dug his fingers deeper into the loam, grounding himself in all ways, and took a few slow, deep breaths. These waking nightmares were rarer than the dreaming ones, fortunately; at night, there was less of a chance he'd hurt anyone. He'd been very lucky just now. He could have damaged a building, the livestock, or worse. Rodrik hadn't come by today. What if he had decided to show at that exact dizzying moment, had stolen upon Anduin in that quiet way of his?

Anduin got to his feet, drank deeply from the waterskin, and wiped his face, then glanced at the road and grimaced. As if on cue, Rodrik was approaching with Anduin's twice-weekly supplies. There was nothing unusual in that, but the sky was already turning lavender.

Anduin rinsed his hands and face and braced himself, hoping he didn't look too distraught. He'd do what he could to make this quick.

"You're later than usual," he said as he began to unload the wagon. "Won't you be late for dinner?"

"Not tonight." Rodrik shot him an impish smile, then carefully climbed out of the vehicle. "I hope you're hungry. We, my young friend, are about to dine on Vera Feldon's world-famous spring vegetable stew and berry pie."

"No, no, that's all right, I don't need—"

Rodrik limped up to Anduin. "Everything came out of the oven less than an hour ago. You're not going to make me go home and tell Vera I didn't feed you, are you?"

There was, of course, no answer other than acquiescence. As

Anduin put away the supplies, Rodrik started to light the fire in the little cottage.

"No," Anduin said. He didn't want to be in a small space right now. "Let's eat outside."

There was a brief pause, then Rodrik nodded, heading out to the fire pit instead. As Anduin emerged from the millhouse, Rodrik called out to him. "You're going to need to set that snare."

"It's all right," Anduin said. "He's fine." As if to confirm it, the fox yipped and trotted over to him. He wouldn't let himself be petted yet, but ever since Anduin began feeding him in the mornings, the fox had taken to following him around during the day. "He catches rats in the millhouse and leaves the chickens alone."

"So far," Rodrik muttered. "Does he have a name?"

"No."

Names had significance. They implied affection, connection. Anduin would not give one to the fox.

The miller placed a small cauldron over the fire and unwrapped the bread and cheese. And, as Anduin had expected, began to talk. First about the bread—it was different, with herbs. Vera was experimenting as the Harvest Festival was coming up in a couple of weeks.

Normal chitchat from Rodrik, yes, but Anduin realized there was something . . . *off* about him tonight. His amiable manner

"I'm not saying
it wasn't worth it, to fight.
But even a war worth fighting
takes its tolls. Some you don't
even know you've paid until
afterward. And some you
just keep paying."

seemed forced. Both men were silent as they ate, but as Anduin ladled another serving, Rodrik asked a question that was both innocent and agonizing.

"Were you . . . in the war?"

Anduin froze and swallowed hard. Oh yes, he had been in the war. In many ways, Anduin felt he had *been* the war. He couldn't speak, but nodded.

"I'm not saying it wasn't worth it, to fight. But even a war worth fighting takes its tolls. Some you don't even know you've paid until afterward. And some you just keep paying."

Anduin stared at the bowl cooling in his lap. He'd been hungry a moment ago, but now the food sat rock-heavy in his stomach. A cold sweat began to grip him.

"Things that you think shouldn't bother you . . . do. Like a fire outside. There was a time when I couldn't even sit here like I'm doing now. Still don't like it much, but it's better." He took a breath, held it, then blew it out slowly. "Breathing like that helps. So does moving your body."

His body, moving without his will. Anduin took a deep breath.

"We were ambushed at our campfire. Three of my friends just suddenly sprouted arrows. Fighting in the dark, trolls so much bigger than we were. Anyone who tried to stand against that—" Rodrik paused. His face seemed pale, even in the fire's glow, and he was trembling. "We ran. We had to. I *know* I had to. But I shouldn't have left the others behind. I . . . dream about it sometimes."

Kingsmourne, glowing icy blue, merciful oblivion ripped away so Anduin could see, understand—his own hand *on the hilt,* his own blow *pulling forth the sigil*—

"Took me a long time to even tell Vera—"

Anduin sprang up, the bowl falling from his lap. "You better get back, it's late," he said, his voice broken. He turned and strode off, breaking into a run as he went, just like the fox who followed him. Running from Rodrik's pain and truth—and his own.

"The Harvest Festival is tomorrow," Rodrik said two weeks later, after Anduin had finished loading the cart with several bags of flour. "Vera makes a special dessert for it. Served hot right out of the oil and covered with sugar."

Anduin knew the treat. Suddenly, he could smell the oil, the sugar, and his mouth watered.

Varian, king, father, his large, strong hands covered with the sweet powder. "You can lick your fingers here, son. Manners are for formal dinners, not festivals." The taste hitting his tongue, the sound of laughter and music—

Anduin, the diplomat,
the peacemaker, who once
would have gracefully deflected
the words and promised all
was well, couldn't speak.

Rodrik must have seen him flinch. "No need to come, of course, but you'd be welcome."

"We'll see," Anduin managed. They both knew what that meant.

The wagon was ready to go, but Rodrik, in the front seat, did not slap the reins to signal the horse to depart. Anduin tensed.

"Jerek . . . about our last conversation . . ."

Shame washed through Anduin. "I'm sorry, I—"

"No, no, *I'm* sorry. That was my error."

Confused, Anduin stayed silent. Rodrik shook his balding head sadly. "I see me in you, Jerek. In those times when you get angry or can't breathe or just plain want me gone. I recognize it when you shake and sweat and seem to see things I can't. I wanted you to know I don't judge anybody for what war, or anything else, might have done to them, so I told you my story. Some of it, at any rate. And it made you think of your own at a moment when you weren't expecting to."

Anduin, the diplomat, the peacemaker, who once would have gracefully deflected the words and promised all was well, couldn't speak.

Rodrik held out a folded piece of parchment. "I wrote down some thoughts about my own experience. Some things I've learned that might help you. You don't have to read it, and you don't have to say a word. But if you do—you know I'm here."

Anduin swallowed. He stepped forward, alert and cautious, just like the fox had been at first. The parchment crackled slightly as he took it.

Rodrik visibly relaxed and gave him one of his easy smiles. "I'll make sure Vera saves some pastries for you," he said, and clicked his tongue. The horse blew, tossed her mane, and began to trot down the road.

Anduin looked at the letter, put it in his pocket unread, and lifted a sack of grain.

The following day was perfect for an autumn harvest festival, crisp and bright, the sun's warmth staving off the slight chill that heralded the winter to come. Anduin spent most of the morning inside the millhouse, tinkering with the gears. He finally finished and stepped outside.

Black smoke roiled in the distance as lighter smoke stained the sky. The festival. Rodrik. A deep instinct—the need to help—drove Anduin's next movements, and before he quite realized what he was doing, he had leaped atop the startled wagon horse and was urging her on to top speed.

Toward his friend—and his family. Anduin had steeled himself for a scene of chaos. Rodrik had mentioned hot oil—there must have been an accident, a fire spreading from a makeshift hearth. Anduin could, and *would*, help.

It was nothing so innocuous.

An utter inferno raged. Through gaps in the smoke, Anduin saw that some festival structures were already consumed and others were fiery skeletons on the verge of collapse. Even the banners were ablaze, and Anduin stared, frozen, almost hypnotized, watching a flag of House Stormstrong curl and twist, blackening as flames licked it.

Shapes on the ground—bodies, Anduin realized. One just there, burned, charred, meat left too long on a spit. Screams on his left as two shapes, a blanket draped over them, emerged from the black smoke.

Waiting, watching, safe in Stormwind, while a World Tree burned and too many tried to flee through too few portals—

Anduin, startled, cried out just as his terrified horse reared and threw him. His head struck something hard. Everything went white for a moment, then dissolved into flashes of light, like stars. Anduin tried to rise, but the world was spinning. He couldn't see the two figures anymore, but a third stumbled out of the enveloping smoke. Anduin thought he saw someone behind her, quickly glimpsed and quickly gone. Perhaps not even there. The woman clutched an infant, shielding it as best she could—

THE CALLING

The child, borne by a queen, brought to a priestess, the last survivor—

The woman dropped like a stone. The baby cried, coughing. More shouting. Laughter. Screaming.

Pain thundered in his skull. Anduin clapped his hands to his ears, the gesture slicking his fingers with blood. He looked around wildly, trying and failing to focus, the coughing that racked his body only increasing the agony, the stench of blood and the cacophony of slaughter making his heart slam against his chest.

The stars started to fade, and Anduin now glimpsed wagons filled with food and supplies waiting out of the reach of the greedy flames. The drivers finally allowed the maddened horses a chance to run, and the wagons careened off. A few of the raiders lingered, barely visible through the smoke, wanting more sport, and then—

Rodrik.

Anduin shook violently. His limbs struggled to obey him, and his head threatened unconsciousness as he tried to rise. So he crawled, keeping his face close to the ground, trying to breathe. Everything in him shouted, *Run! Run!*

But he clenched his teeth against another scream and willed himself to keep going.

Impossibly, more folk emerged from the fire. Some stumbled, as if someone had pushed them from behind. How were they

"I can't," he rasped, over
and over, his voice a sob.
He reached out again, to lay
his hands on the wound,
to form the prayer—

It won't come. Not to me.
Not anymore.

still alive? Soot, smoke, and tears stung Anduin's eyes and he was glad of it, glad of the pain, the blurring, so he could not see what horrors the fire had wrought upon the figures.

The baby was still crying, coughing, and a someone swooped down to pick it up and flee. Another figure emerged from the billowing black cloud, burned, but not as badly as others. Something about how it—how *he*—moved the right leg . . .

"Rodrik!" Anduin tried to shout, but all that came out was a ragged sound.

I'm not too late. I can help him. I—

Rodrik crumpled to the ground.

Anduin had no memory of how he crossed the distance between him and his fallen friend. The next thing he knew, he was kneeling beside the miller, staring at the blackened flesh, the blue eyes in the sooty face, the well of blood pumping up between his own fingers as he pressed to stanch the flood, to call—

He gasped, pulled his hands back, his body shaking. He couldn't help Rodrik. Not now.

Anduin, do something. Do something—

"*I can't,*" he rasped, over and over, his voice a sob. He reached out again, to lay his hands on the wound, to form the prayer—

It won't come. Not to me. Not anymore.

Again, he snatched his useless hands back, curling them into fists and pounding them on his thighs with all the force of his rage and helplessness and loathing. "I'm sorry . . . I'm so sorry . . ."

A whisper. "It's all right . . ."

Anduin shook his head. Rodrik's hand twitched and Anduin took it, his heart tearing itself apart as Rodrik cried out at the touch. The dying man gripped all the harder. "Family . . . in town—" A violent bout of coughing threatened to tear him apart as blood and specks of ash burst from his mouth. It took the last of his energy, but even so, Rodrik fought to speak. Anduin stilled him, able to at least grant him peace here, at the end.

"I will take care of them," Anduin said. "I will, I promise . . ."

Rodrik heard him. His taut, tormented body eased. He closed his eyes and was gone.

Ben Feldon had his father's eyes. Also, his father's old war pistol, which was now aimed at the stranger who stood at the doorstep.

Anduin, hands raised, was acutely aware of the picture he presented: his clothing filthy with ashes and wet with blood. Rodrik's blood. Rodrik, whom he had wrapped in a singed blanket and placed down so gently before knocking on the Feldons' door.

"My name is Jerek. From the mill."

Fortunately, Ben recognized the name and lowered the pistol. He too bore signs of the fire, a minor burn on one arm and a singed shirt. They must have escaped, while Rodrik had remained behind.

"Roddy?"

A woman rushed up, looking past him, hoping against hope to see a beloved face. *Vera.* Her black hair was turning gray, but Anduin observed that her face was remarkably unlined . . . until her gaze fell on her husband's body. Realization spread over her face, the pain aging her, dimming her light as she sank down beside the corpse, placed a hand on the still form, and bowed her head.

For a moment, Anduin thought he couldn't keep the wall up. But he knew that if it came down, something inside him would collapse like the burning structures at the festival, in flames and beyond repair.

"Thank you, child." Vera's voice shook, but it was kind. "Bless you for bringing him. He . . . did promise he'd come home."

"Why didn't he let me go with him?" Ben's voice was full of pain and anger.

"He wanted us to be safe."

"We could have *all* been safe, but he just *had* to—" Ben's face crumpled and he turned away.

Rodrik, the soldier, who had been ambushed at a campfire. Who, this time, had decided he couldn't leave anyone behind.

Anduin heard the urgent thump of small running feet, and a little girl appeared at the door. Her hair was braided with now-drooping peacebloom flowers, her soot-smudged face clean only where her tears had run.

"Daddy?"

"Oh, Cynda, honey, no . . ."

I failed you. All of you.

The wall inside Anduin trembled.

Rodrik had wished to be buried near the cliff where he and Vera had pledged themselves to each other years ago, when they were only a little older than Ben.

Anduin dug the grave himself; there was no need to trouble anyone else, and he wanted to do it.

As he worked, he thought of his belongings, far below the six feet of earth he would move. He would never know if the Light would have saved Rodrik and had to live with the knowledge that he had been too afraid to ask. Anything he could do, large or small, to help the bereaved family, he would, except for one thing: he would not attend the funeral. He could not bear to be near anyone wielding the Light. Not now. Perhaps not ever.

That day, he walked. The fox followed, Anduin's little shadow. He didn't return until twilight, to make sure everyone was long gone. To his surprise, there was a box at the cottage door. A small slip of parchment read: *For you, Jerek. Thank you.* The box was full of bread, cheese, vegetables, and some meat wrapped in waxed fabric—even scraps for the fox.

He picked up a piece. "Hey. Fox," he said, and fed him the morsel.

The note reminded Anduin of the one Rodrik had left him, forgotten until this moment. He retrieved it and looked at it for a moment.

Jerek:

We've both known war. It does things to you. You've got a right to whatever you feel. Mad, sad, scared . . . I've felt all that and then some.

I know you better than you might think. It's clear how much you care about doing a good job with the mill. I see your patience and good character in how you treat that fox. A man who'll take time to be kind to animals, especially after what I think you've been through, is rare. And his heart's still good, whatever he thinks.

It helped me to talk with Vera, and it was my hope you'd talk to me. If not, I hope someday you do find someone you trust. Because if you keep a lid on a boiling pot, someone's going to get hurt, and it might not be you.

I guess I'll close with this: Sometimes we have to do terrible things. And sometimes terrible things are done to us. Neither makes us bad people, but we can't run forever. If you can't believe in your own worth right this moment, find someone who does. They'll hold that knowledge safe for you till you're ready to see it too.

And when the darkness grabs you and you feel like you'll never, ever be free of it, know you have a chance and a choice every single day to look it in the eye and call it a liar. Some days, you can't make that choice. But another day, maybe you can.

Eat Vera's good food. Swim in the sea and sleep and work. Do a little good when you can, how you can, for who you can. And come have dinner with us one of these days.

—R

THE CALLING

Ben wanted to take over his father's task of bringing grain to the mill, but Anduin would not let him. Instead, he came into town himself for supplies. It was the least he could do for them. For Rodrik.

On this first trip, Vera insisted he come into the bakery for tea and small pastries. She wanted him to understand what had happened. Word of the area's bounty had reached the ears of some raiders, she said.

"Rats on ships. I tell you, Jerek, there's no monster in the ocean's deep crueler than the ones that sail its surface. Roddy brought us home in the wagon, then went back to save as many others as he could. Said he wasn't going to run this time." She bit her lip. "If . . . if we did have to lose him, I hope he was able to . . . before—"

"He was," Anduin said quietly. "He did."

He saw her brow relax, only a little, and knew the words had given her a little bit of peace.

Over time, a new rhythm and routine took form. Anduin still worked the mill, but at dusk, more often than not, he would sit beside his friend's grave. The fox accompanied him, nestling against him. Sometimes Anduin would speak, as if Rodrik were still there, listening. Quiet confessions, questions that Rodrik would never answer; other times, angry outbursts. Or he'd reread the letter and remember to breathe.

On his visits to town, Anduin would occasionally help Ben with paperwork or loading and unloading the wagons. Now and then, Vera asked for assistance kneading the dough. After a while, Anduin realized she'd sneakily taught him how to bake. She and Ben wanted to talk about Rodrik, which Anduin resisted at first. But over time he realized . . . he *wanted* to hear those stories. They were little ones, mostly—a brilliant quip at the right time, patience with a child's rebelliousness, a Hallow's End costume gone awry. Only Cynda seemed disinclined to talk about her father. Vera confided to Anduin that she was glad that Cynda had been so young when it happened. "Less to miss," Vera said with a sad smile.

But Anduin had often visited Stormwind City's orphanage. He had spent time with refugees who had fled to his city after their home had burned. Intimately familiar with the strange ways of grief and guilt, he wasn't so sure about Vera's statement. He wanted to believe she was right, but that fragile hope was dashed one deceptively calm morning, along with a teapot Cynda grabbed and hurled to the stone floor.

"Cynda!" Vera shouted. "That was a wedding gift from your father!"

"I know!" Cynda shrieked back. "He's not here to care about

it, so why should you? *He* didn't care about *us*!" She seized one of the matching teacups and hurled it to the floor as well, deftly eluding her mother's grasp and racing outside.

"Cynda!" Vera cried, starting after her.

"Let her go," Anduin said, and Vera turned, looking at him sharply. "I know what she said is hurtful, but . . . let her feel what she needs to."

Vera softened.

Surprising himself and her both, Anduin continued. "My mother died when I was a baby. And . . . my father . . ." His throat was tight, but something inside him pushed to keep going.

"Something happened to him, and he left when I was around Cynda's age. He came back. Things were better, but . . . it's hard to understand complicated situations when you're so young. She'll come back, and she'll talk to you when she can. She knows you—" *love her* was what he wanted to say, but couldn't.

Vera's sweet smile returned. "You're right. Hard to remember to breathe when you're in the thick of it. You're a good man, Jerek. Roddy was right about you. You're welcome here anytime."

He stammered his thanks and departed.

On his next visit, he brought the fox with him. The animal was skittish, but Anduin knew a way around it. Plucking a berry from a bowl on the table, he said, "Hey. Fox." That got Anduin's attention, and the berry rapidly vanished into the fox's mouth.

"I like berries too," Cynda said, delighted, and quickly emulated both the fox and Anduin, popping some berries into her mouth while offering a handful to the appreciative creature.

"No berry pie today, I guess, but it's worth it to see her smile," Vera said, smiling herself. "Come sit with me for a moment, Jerek. Tell me what you think of this. It's got honey and flowers in it."

The little roll looked small in his large palm. It smelled wonderful, and for the first time in a while, Anduin felt real pleasure at the flavor. He finished it in two bites. Vera's eyes crinkled, and she handed him another one.

"He likes you," Anduin said to Cynda. The fox was presenting his white belly for the girl to rub. When she did, the fox squirmed with delight, emitting a high-pitched, squeaky cackle.

"He's laughing!" Cynda said, laughing along with him. Still grinning, she looked up at Anduin, and her smile turned a bit sad.

"Mama told me about your mama and papa. I'm sorry."

Surprised, Anduin looked over at Vera.

"It helped," Vera said. "For her to hear that."

"I miss Papa a lot," Cynda said. She was still petting the fox. "Mama says that won't go away, but it'll get easier. And we have each other." She looked at Anduin, sad, but smiling. "Don't we?"

Anduin was about to reply when he realized that she was including him.

Oh no, little one.
No, I don't. One day,
I'll let you down too, just
as I have everyone else.

Oh no, little one. No, I don't. One day, I'll let you down too, just as I have everyone else.

Time passed. Anduin worked, keeping his hands busy. The nightmares dwindled further, becoming rare. The anxiety that sometimes descended out of nowhere eased its grip on his soul. And the flashbacks, those shattering, raw moments of hellish memories seeming far too real, all but ceased.

In the end, as a part of him had always known would happen, it did not last.

They would die at his hands. His friends. Those who believed in him, who were trying to save him. He'd failed them.

The smoke, the infant crying, calling for help as best it could—

Anduin bolted up. The crying was coming from the fox, who whimpered and pawed at him. His ears were flat against his head.

Something was very wrong. Anduin shook off the dream almost physically, stroking the animal to reassure him as he got to his feet and looked out the window.

In the south, a thin gray pillar stretched upward.

Smoke.

"No," Anduin whispered. His legs trembled.

THE CALLING

He couldn't do fail them. Not again. He couldn't bear it. And yet still his legs were moving, dreading every twitch of muscle. Racing now to the wagon horse, racing now to the bundle he'd buried. Even as he couldn't unwrap the sword for fear of gripping its hilt. What if he couldn't stop? What if he took too much pleasure in hefting it once more? There was no way to be safe, to ensure he stayed in control.

And still he rode for the village. For Vera and Ben and little Cynda and the promise he'd made to a man who understood him, who trusted him, when he had no reason to. When he couldn't know what Anduin had done, how he'd so deeply betrayed his every charge and duty.

At the festival, the smoke had been black and oily and the buildings all but gone by the time Anduin had arrived. This time, everything was different.

Only a few structures were burning, and the raiders were clearly only beginning their assault. The cacophony was the same, though: Laughter. Screams. Violence.

Anduin clenched his teeth, blocking the rush of fear as if with a shield. He slipped easily off the horse and sent it to safety. His right hand clenched tightly, his left coming to join it as, for the first time since he had left the realms of Death, Anduin Llane Wrynn lifted high his father's sword.

Shalamayne.

So much more than a simple weapon, gloriously crafted, each part of it in harmony despite its origin as two individually powerful blades. Anduin stepped forward, grim-faced, devoid of armor but hoisting this sword out of legend. This sword whose purpose he had so utterly failed, which he now lifted in hope of redemption.

One of the pirates turned and paled. His eyes grew enormous—

The wide eyes, wider in terror—

For a terrible instant, Anduin froze. He couldn't breathe.

The brigand started to smile, lifting a cutlass.

Shalamayne came down in a deceptively graceful arc, mortally wounding the man.

Its perfect balance made its wielding easy, almost effortless. There was little it would not cut through and few foes it could not fell. The brutality of it stole his breath, but then muscle memory took over. Anduin struck again and again, Shalamayne almost singing in his hands, as if it rejoiced in being used once more at the defense of innocents. He and the sword, for this moment, were one.

Blood spattered on his face, warm and wet; it stung his eyes, seeped into his mouth. He wiped his lips and pressed on. Another fell, and another. He ceased to count, and time ceased to matter. He moved as if in a dance, without thinking, feeling only the power of his arm and hearing only the song of the sword. Anduin lunged, burying Shalamayne almost to its hilt, then yanked it free only to parry blows again and again.

The enemy was on the ground, but Anduin continued to fight. The sword lifted and descended—

A muffled voice tried to cut through the chaos. A word. Nonsense and nothing to him now, in this scarlet span of time.

A name. Not his, no . . . but he knew it . . .

"Jerek! *Jerek!*"

Anduin shouted incoherently, lifting Shalamayne to strike—

Cynda stood, staring up at him, her mouth open in a look of shock. But she was not afraid of him. Unthinkably, foolishly, *she was not afraid*, and she squeezed his arm, saying things he could not understand but were gentle and comforting.

Anduin . . .

The call was quiet, but this voice was not that of the child before him. It slammed into his being, shattering his thoughts into a kaleidoscope of agony and brilliant colors. It was a song with words he understood yet did not recognize, which vibrated along every nerve of his body. And the singer, the speaker, knew his true name.

Anduin, it whispered, the softness laced with pain. An image filled his mind: what seemed to be a sun, white-hot at its heart, with hues of yellow and magenta flickering along the edges.

Anduin. So beautiful, this voice, this vision, but he understood that what he beheld was in danger. That at some point—perhaps soon—it might explode.

It was calling him away. He was needed.

No, he pleaded, to who or what he did not know. *I'm needed here. Please.*

Anduin . . . came the implacable reply, and he could feel the voice's sorrow and torment.

The touch on his arm galvanized him, and he started, blinking, the vision retreating. Cynda was still there, her expression one of concern. "Are you all right, Jerek?"

Anduin looked at the bodies littered around him. At Vera and Ben, who huddled together, looking at him with sympathy and gratitude, at the shocked faces of the townsfolk. There was no more screaming or shouting. Anduin had brought silence. How many had he killed, without even—?

He stared at Shalamayne, seeing it as if for the first time.

There was no light moving in the blade's curve.

No gold, but at least, blessedly, no icy blue.

The sword clattered to the street as Anduin dropped to his knees, gasping, staring at Cynda. "Why did you come to me? I . . . I could have *killed* you."

She smiled a little. "Because I knew you wouldn't."

Anduin's eyes filled with tears.

"I wish I could stay," Anduin said to Rodrik, to the wind, to himself.

He had cleaned the blood off Shalamayne, then retrieved pieces of his old armor from the cave where they had lain undisturbed for what felt like a lifetime. He had tidied the cottage, fed the goats and chickens, and organized the sacks of grain. Now he sat beside his friend's grave, clad in armor, with Shalamayne on his right and the fox, eyes closed as Anduin scratched his ears, on his left.

"But I know you would understand. Thank you. For everything you've taught me."

He gripped Rodrik's letter, then tucked it into his pocket.

Suddenly, the fox sat up, alert, and gazed toward the road before running toward it. Anduin thought he had made his goodbyes to the Feldons after Cynda, in her innocent faith, had broken the spell that violence had held on him. For the moment. But he was not altogether surprised to see Rodrik's wagon coming up the road with all three Feldons on it.

"You're a fool if you think we're letting you go without proper food and supplies," Vera said as Ben brought the wagon to a halt.

Anduin stood. "I thank you, but I'll be traveling light."

He knew nothing
about what awaited him—
who or what was calling to him
or what it wanted. Only that
it was in pain and needed help,
and so he would go.

"My pastries are light," Vera countered.

Anduin could not disagree.

"Jerek," Ben said, "that sword . . ."

"Plenty of wandering adventurers fight with swords, Ben," Vera said swiftly. "You know how your father hated anyone prying."

"It's all right, Ben." And, oddly, it was. It didn't matter now if someone recognized him, or Shalamayne.

"Can't you stay, Jerek?" Cynda asked, racing to him. When he shook his head, she said, "Will you ever come back?"

"I cannot stay," he said. He knew nothing about what awaited him—who or what was calling to him or what it wanted. Only that it was in pain and needed help, and so he would go. "I—" His voice cracked as he spoke. The next thing he knew, Cynda had thrown herself at him, hugging him tight. Anduin froze, then, gently, awkwardly, patted her on the back.

"Let the poor boy go, Cynda," Vera said. The girl did so, reluctantly. Vera handed him a bag heavy with food, water, potions, and other supplies. Anduin accepted it with a nod, then picked up Shalamayne wrapped in his cloak.

"I don't know what you're going toward, but I wish you safety and joy, if you can find it."

He couldn't speak, just nodded, then quickly turned, knowing that if he lingered but a moment longer, he might not be able to leave at all. He had scarcely gone three steps when a red blur sped toward him and nearly knocked him down.

Anduin broke.

He knelt and pulled Fox—*"Fox," not the* fox *or a* fox, *not anymore; of course he'd gone and named him and been too foolish to see it*—into his arms. Fox licked the tears from his face as Anduin held him tightly. Where he was going, Fox must not follow. To endure whatever awaited him, Anduin needed to know that this family, Fox among them, was safe and at peace. And so he picked him up and bore him to Cynda, placing him in the girl's arms.

"Hold Fox tight," Anduin told her. "Don't let him follow me. He's yours now."

Cynda's eyes filled with tears, and she nodded, clutching the squirming creature who cried piteously, marking the girl's bare arms with welts from his claws.

Alone, Anduin faced the road. His feet were heavy, but he wasn't running anymore. He was being called—away from people he cared for, yes, but toward something that needed his help. He still didn't trust himself, but the people he cared for did. He would let that be enough, while he struggled to find peace with his past.

In the meantime, he would follow that call, whatever—whoever—was waiting for him.

A WHISPER OF WARNING

DELILAH S. DAWSON

The afternoon sun filtered through the crimson leaves overhead as Alleria Windrunner walked the path toward Silvermoon City. In times past, happier times, she might have flown or used a portal to appear inside the city walls, but as it was, she approached warily, as if nearing a sleeping beast that did not wake gently. Once, she had defended these walls, these people. But now?

Now, to many, she was the source of danger.

Funny how she had faced the most terrifying monsters, demons, the very worst of the Horde, and yet here the thought of passing through a simple gate filled her with trepidation.

Turn around and leave. This place is full of enemies. Everybody hates you.

Alleria ignored the whispers. When they were this foolish, it was easy.

Alleria ignored
the whispers. When
they were this foolish,
it was easy.

A WHISPER OF WARNING

Her boots carried her forward. Her mission could not be stopped by her own fears, much less by those that came from her connection to the Void. Recently, Khadgar had summoned her to Dalaran, where he'd asked her to investigate something called the Dark Heart: an object that Iridikron had found within Aberrus and given to a being known as the Harbinger. For all his wisdom, Khadgar knew nothing more; regardless, Alleria was accustomed to acting on vague reports and would soon uncover the meaning of this new threat—and end it.

But first, she had to do something that worried her far more.

She had to speak with her son, Arator.

Whatever was coming, whatever the Dark Heart portended, she had to warn him to stay away from it. Despite their estranged relationship of late, despite her spending time in the Rift to be away from Stormwind City and constantly on back-to-back missions, she could only hope her son would listen. And so she stood at the gates to the city her son called home and watched a familiar figure stalk her way.

"Alleria Windrunner. Have you forgotten that you were banished from Silvermoon?"

"Lor'themar," she responded with less respect than he surely preferred. Her sights landed on his gleaming armor. "Have you been demoted to guard duty? Such a petty task seems below the station of Regent Lord of Quel'Thalas."

He raised a long white eyebrow. "When there is a significant threat that requires my attention, I attend."

"I am no threat, old friend. At least, I would assume that if you found me threatening, you would not have invited me to your wedding. Not that your wedding was uneventful—or without its threats. I never did get to taste that exquisite lavender cake."

"I can direct you to the baker, if you'd like to commission one similar." Lor'themar opened a gate and stood there looking somber. "Why are you here, Alleria?"

The city shone behind him, glimmering white walls with red tiled roofs and gilded frames, the sun glinting off windows. A place so familiar, even if subtle differences showed in the process of reconstruction after the ravages of the Scourge. A place she had known all her life. A place she was no longer welcome.

"I came to see my son. I am leaving shortly on a mission, and I wish to say goodbye."

"An admirable reason to cross our threshold. But remember this, Alleria. Your welcome, if one can call it that, extends only so long as the sun touches Silvermoon. Once night falls, you must leave."

These were the same conditions upon which she had agreed to attend his wedding in Suramar—one day, and no later. Even

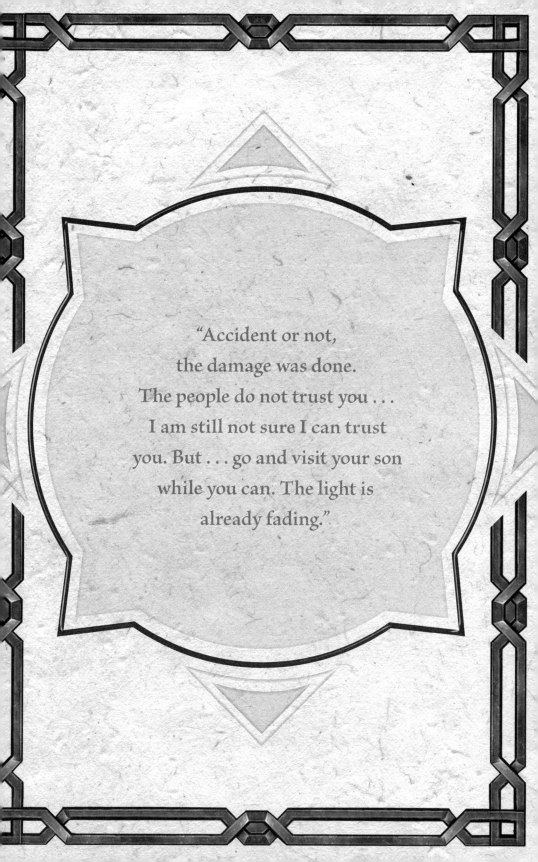

"Accident or not,
the damage was done.
The people do not trust you . . .
I am still not sure I can trust
you. But . . . go and visit your son
while you can. The light is
already fading."

as a former ranger-captain of Silvermoon and a hero, she knew the city would treat her as they treated all enemies if she were to overstay her welcome.

Alleria's chest tightened. "I am no enemy. You must understand, what happened at the Sunwell was an accident—"

Lor'themar waved a hand, cutting her off; few others in Azeroth would dare to do so. "Accident or not, the damage was done. The people do not trust you . . . I am still not sure I can trust you. But . . . go and visit your son while you can. The light is already fading."

Now return to the Sunwell and finish our communion.

You owe Lor'themar nothing.

Claim what is yours. Destroy him and take this place!

He gestured to his guards to follow her, then strode away as Alleria's hands went to fists, creaking in their gloves. They were both right, she and Lor'themar, and she loathed that. She was culpable for damaging the heart of her people's culture, but she truly had not known that just being near the Sunwell might allow her Void nature to corrupt its magic.

Being in the presence of that ancient, magical fount had soothed her soul at first, like standing in full sun after an eternity of dark and stormy nights. She had felt the power flow into her, filling her with Light—and then it were as if she herself had become a portal, and creatures of the Void spilled out like pus from a wound. And then she had risked her life to fight the catastrophe she had unleashed.

But it was not enough to end what she had inadvertently started. As much as she hated to admit it, in many ways, she was a threat to everything she loved—which explained why she had been keeping her own loved ones at a distance, as she had explained to Khadgar during her visit.

Still, she had ties here, old and new, and the Regent Lord had at least honored that history.

She ignored the whispers—from the Void and from her own conscience—and refocused on her goal, even as Lor'themar's guards fanned out around her, keeping their distance. She would be unable to walk freely, but that changed nothing. They were there to stop her from harming the city, but that had never been her intention.

The streets of Silvermoon were being recobbled, but they still felt the same under her silver-chased boots, were still imbued with the same beauty and magic. The trees lining the path had pale bark and branches with eternally orange leaves, and the large white columns were right where she remembered them to be, rising tall on either side of her. Alleria knew her way here, and as she walked, memories floated up, layers upon layers like watercolor paint built up in many washes.

As she walked, the residents of Silvermoon came into sharper focus, and their unease was palpable. Spotting her, people retreated through open doors and disappeared down alleys. Faces with perked ears appeared in windows before drapes were quickly drawn.

Indeed, Lor'themar was right. The people did not trust her. They actively seemed to fear her. Word must have spread about the Sunwell—spread, and perhaps grown in the spreading like some foul, destructive fungus. Or perhaps it was the heavy white-and-silver armor on her left arm and the enormous bow that never left her side. She was a warrior through and through, and commoners often reacted to her like rabbits stilling in the shadow of a hawk.

How easily they turn on you. Like your true love has turned on you.

You repulse Turalyon.

Your son fears you too.

Unleash what repels them. Destroy them.

Destroy all the unworthy insects here. Seize your power!

Alleria's steps hastened. Perhaps it looked the same, but this place no longer felt like any sort of home. In truth, she was not sure what *home* even meant to her anymore.

She strolled past scaffolding where carpenters and masons worked to rebuild various structures, and toward a row of houses, a place she had only ever heard about from Arator. Even though he was a man grown, she still saw in him the wailing bundle she'd handed off to her sister Vereesa when she'd journeyed beyond the Dark Portal, before fate had turned her life upside down. Since her return from the Twisting Nether, she had kept her distance, fearful her connection to the Void might harm her son. And so her relationship with him had withered.

But with every heartbeat pounding in her chest, she would see their bond mended, as much as it could be, and impart her warning that he needed to stay safe, here in the broken but cherished city she had walked as a child. She would fight as she always had, for the safety of her son and for the world they shared, and he would carry forward her hope for a time when this world would know peace.

Finally, she stood before the blood-red door. The golden door knocker was shaped like a phoenix, its worn metal suggesting that at some point visitors had been welcome here. Through the open window, she heard a voice that made her heart race and her eyes light up. What was her love doing here? She paused a moment, like a good ranger, to see what awaited her on the battlefield.

"Did I ever tell you about how your mother and I introduced the elekk to the Army of Light?" Turalyon said. "We'd worked with them on Draenor, and we suspected their tenacity, hardiness, and intelligence would make them boons as mounts."

"I seem to recall that you've mentioned it."

Now he himself was
a Knight of the Silver Hand.

He had tasted war.

He was a man.

And still, he barely knew her—

And she him.

Hearing that voice, and the subtle but fond annoyance in it, Alleria's heart melted.

Her son.

Arator.

Once an infant in her arms, barely visible through her tears as she said goodbye, knowing that leaving was the only way to keep him safe.

Then a toddler with a sword who thought war a grand thing.

Then a boy sitting upon the shoulders of a Knight of the Silver Hand, looking up at a statue of the mother he barely knew in the Valley of Heroes, feeling the warmth of her love beamed across the universe in the Light and reaching for her graven face.

Now he himself was a Knight of the Silver Hand.

He had tasted war.

He was a man.

And still, he barely knew her—

And she him.

You will never know him. He will see you as a monster, a traitor. An enemy.

"We've had so many grand adventures," Turalyon continued with a rasping chuckle.

"Where do you think she is now?" she heard Arator ask.

The question filled her with unease. Perhaps it was reasonable to stand outside the open window as they spoke of elekk, but Alleria would not eavesdrop as they spoke of her. Not only because she might betray herself with a gasp or a sigh and be caught, but also because she might hear something she desperately did not want to hear.

"You know I love her dearly, but your mother . . . can't be contained."

She froze again, and a smile tugged at the corner of her mouth.

"I know you miss her."

"Of course I do. But . . ."

And just as quickly, her smile faded. She and Turalyon had been taking time apart lately, leaning into their respective work. She on her missions, Turalyon off to attend council meetings.

"She thinks she's a danger to us," Arator said sadly. "And you think so too."

See? They do *fear you.*

They should *fear you.*

Kill them.

Alleria's hand reached for the door. She knew it was wrong to keep eavesdropping. But while she could not picture a life without Turalyon, she knew he found her Void nature strange, though he had never admitted it and likely never would. Now, she wished to hear him say it plainly. She herself found it strange, but it lay between them, an uncrossable gulf that they neither could cross, for all that she would've welcomed the opportunity to be honest about the chaos that lived within her.

"Thinking won't bring her home," Turalyon said. "Now, did I ever tell you how an elekk that feeds exclusively on orchids produces—"

"Taladorian cheese. You can keep dodging the topic, but I would like to know the truth."

A weighty pause.

"Well, I suppose you have more important matters with which to concern yourself than cheese."

"I am not a child, Father. You cannot distract me. Please, I beg you: tell me of my mother. You so seldom speak of her."

Another sigh.

You detest Turalyon. He is weak.

End him. He will only cause pain. He will never understand.

Your true power lies beyond him.

"Your mother is the love of my life, and she is . . . a complicated creature."

Alleria could take no more. She grasped the summer-warm brass of the door knocker and looked to the sky as she knocked three times. The sun was golden now but was swiftly arcing toward the horizon. Soon, the sky would fade to periwinkle and pink, and the stars would begin to wink out. She did not have the time she needed, so she had to make the time she had count.

"Were you expecting someone, son?" she heard Turalyon ask. "One of the Breezeblossom twins dropping off a jar of starflower honey, perhaps?"

"Father, please. I am expecting no one, and no one should be expecting me. My thoughts are with my fellow Knights, not with some paltry dalliance."

Their son sounded like his robes were suddenly too tight and strangling him. When Arator opened the door, his cheeks were pink and he was clearly doing his best to look serious.

Seeing her, he failed.

His jaw dropped and hope glowed in his golden eyes. As a baby, they'd been green like hers, but sometime in their long, long time apart, they had shifted color. Alleria did not mind this change; to her, he had always shone like the sun.

"Mother!" he said with a surprised smile.

"My son." She wanted to hug him, but he was enormous and fully armored in shades of gold, same as he'd looked when last she'd seen him only a few months prior. Instead, she reached out a hand to cup his cheek. "I cannot believe that I am saying this, but my boy, you need a good shave."

Arator laughed and stepped back so that she could enter the chamber.

The moment the door was shut behind her, the whispers were but a distant hum.

A WHISPER OF WARNING

She turned toward Turalyon like a magnet finding true north. He had not changed in the past months. In all their years together—centuries spanning realms and worlds and dimensions—he had always been beautiful to her. His new scars only served to highlight his strength and tenacity, and she could feel the pull of him, although she fought it.

"My love," he said, warmly if a bit warily.

Alleria could deny it no longer. Perhaps things were strange between them, but each time they parted, they knew not if they would see each other again.

She moved to embrace him but stopped, and the short distance between them seemed to span for great lengths. "I have missed you," she said, her voice low.

"And I you."

Their son watched, expecting them to hug, or at least touch. But neither did.

Alleria could see the hurt in Turalyon's eyes, could feel the same longing to sink into each other and take the comfort that had long fed them both.

"I was in town to consult with Liadrin on a matter and wished to keep a low profile," Turalyon continued with a smile. "Will you be staying for a while, or is your sojourn as brief as mine?"

She gazed into his eyes; she wanted him to see that she was

not pleased to be leaving so soon. "You know me well. I am soon to depart on a mission for Khadgar. I would stay here with you both longer, but Lor'themar made it clear that my presence in Silvermoon is not welcome. I must leave by nightfall or threaten any goodwill he still has for the bond we once shared."

Turalyon nodded. "Shall I join you on this journey?"

Of course she considered it. But the more she learned about the Void and the more she used her Void powers, the more uncomfortable the paladin grew in her presence. Like he had said, she was a complicated creature.

He will never accept your true nature.

Alleria knew that if Turalyon could hear the voices that clawed at her psyche, he would either push her away forever or spend the rest of his life trying to fix her, possibilities that were equally repugnant. She loved him for exactly who he was and sometimes wondered if he loved her merely out of habit and stubbornness. She was changing and evolving into something new, but Turalyon was hardening into who he was and had always been. He didn't need to know that.

"This is a quest I must undertake alone, but my son may join me on a brief walk before I depart," she said at last.

"An excellent idea." Turalyon all but shone with hope. "I am certain you two have much to discuss."

"I should like to see Silvermoon during the golden hour, if

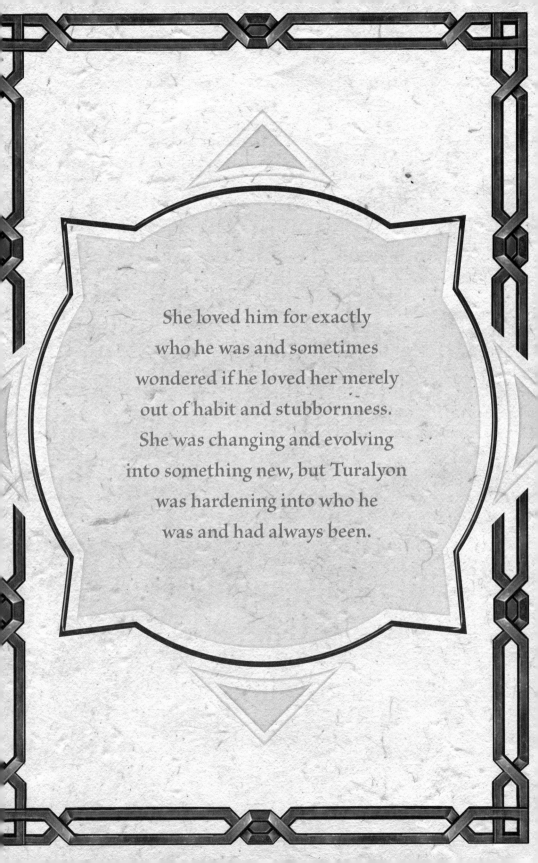

She loved him for exactly
who he was and sometimes
wondered if he loved her merely
out of habit and stubbornness.
She was changing and evolving
into something new, but Turalyon
was hardening into who he
was and had always been.

Azeroth and her children
deserved to know peace, and
Alleria had spent the better
part of her thousand years
vainly chasing it.

you'll squire me. I have heard the architects are doing a beautiful job with the new construction."

Arator held out his arm, but Alleria did not take it, not yet.

"Perhaps it would be best to shed our armor and walk among the crowd disguised as regular citizens?" she said, eyeing his gargantuan pauldrons. "Those I passed on my way here did not look too fondly on my weaponry. Nor did Lor'themar's guards."

It vaguely annoyed her when her son looked to Turalyon for his opinion.

"Go on and pretend," he said with a chuckle. "Pretend for an afternoon that you are normal. War will not break out in the next hour."

"As you wish." Arator began to unstrap his heavy pauldrons, and Alleria stuffed her own armor and weapons into an enchanted bag. Thus unburdened, she felt light and quick and confident that she still had the resources and skills to handle any threat that might come.

How strange, she thought, *that a mother going for an afternoon stroll with her son should wish to be armed to the teeth.*

Stranger still that she herself was considered the biggest threat here.

Many thought all Windrunners were born to fight, but that was not true. Alleria's father and brother had rarely hefted sword and bow. Some in Silvermoon still lived such a life, believing their walls were enough to keep their city safe. They were wrong, of course, but that did not mean Alleria could not dream of a return to such a time, when she might see her son dance in the glen or put his lips to a merry fife. Azeroth and her children deserved to know peace, and Alleria had spent the better part of her thousand years vainly chasing it.

As Arator continued to remove his armor, Turalyon stepped closer to her, smiling again. "How . . . were your travels?" he asked.

"Fair," she replied. "And matters at Stormwind?"

"The same."

"And what of Silvermoon? Is Greaves still making sugar spindles here? And is Branson still a stuffy, gossipy noble?"

"Truth be told, we are kept too busy for such amusements, but I hope you will see them while out on your walk."

At that, she smiled at him in turn, but with a hint of sadness.

His smile was sad too. He gestured to Arator. "Hurry up, son. Enjoy the sunshine. I know my arguments will not convince your mother to settle down for a while back in Stormwind, but perhaps you can sway her. It would be pleasant, to spend what time we can as a family."

But Alleria could sense the lie wrapped in this truth. It was a charming idea, to be sure, but the reality would involve three people who did not truly know or understand each other, reaching awkwardly for conversation and waiting for the next war. Turalyon might have hoped the young paladin had the power to bring his mother home, but as it turned out, Alleria was the one who would be doing the convincing.

Once Arator had finished removing all his armor, Alleria looked at her son in his simple black robes and felt a rush of pride for her offspring. He married her lithe quickness with Turalyon's sturdy strength, but improved by regal posture and a kind smile. This time when he offered his arm she took it, and he escorted her out of the house.

She looked back at Turalyon briefly, and he waved and mouthed, "I love you."

"Yes, love," she mouthed back. To her great sorrow, she realized that she had gotten better at leaving him than reuniting with him. For a long moment, their eyes locked, and what passed between them was not a sentence or a sonnet, not even a tome, but an entire library of feelings unspoken. So much she wanted to say but didn't know how. So much that could never be said. His eyes begged for her to come home, but he would not ask that sacrifice of her. His yearning tugged at her soul, but at last she had to look away.

Another time.

Another time, they would speak from the heart.

Another time, perhaps, she would stay.

She hated this just as much as he did.

But if they did not part ways and fight their own battles, the world would end—existence would end—and there would be nowhere left to reunite. Thus duty would always take precedence over love; and his understanding of that was one of the reasons she loved him in the first place.

When Alleria returned her focus to Arator, she saw something similar in his face—love, loss, yearning. He had seen the look pass between his parents, witnessed an intimate, intricate moment, and now he had to look away.

"You've chosen a lovely day," he said after clearing his throat.

Outside, the golden hour reigned supreme. Warm sunbeams the color of melted butter arced down through the gently rustling leaves, themselves a blaze of copper and crimson striking all the touches of gold with a triumphant glow. Lavender shadows shifted on the cobblestones and crept up the sides of the newly painted white buildings. Even if she were angry with Lor'themar, Alleria could still see the beauty and style in this place, and she still felt somewhat at home here even if that sense of belonging came with a ticking clock.

"We're being followed," Arator remarked under his breath.

She flicked a glance at the watchful guards. "A condition of my visit. Worry not."

"I shall pretend we are alone, then, despite our entourage."

A WHISPER OF WARNING

Looking up into the sun, Arator rolled up his sleeves, and Alleria was surprised to see tattoos covering his forearms.

"When did you get those?" she said, daring to touch the dark dragon twining up his wrist. On his other arm, the dragon's sunny twin curled in perfect symmetry. One dark, one light.

Arator looked down sheepishly and attempted to pull his sleeves back into place. "Oh, I . . . I mean . . ."

"Your father might mind them, but I do not. They are beautiful."

Relaxing, he rolled up both sleeves and held out his arms so that she could admire the work.

"Someone amazing gave them to me." A lopsided grin.

"Yes. I recognize the style." She returned his grin. She liked this small act of revolt. Proof that even if she had not raised him, he had at least inherited some aspects of her personality. "A little rebellion is good for the soul," she added.

And for a moment, it felt as if they had some common ground, a place where they might begin to build something better. Perhaps to Arator it was just a shared smile and some ink, but Alleria knew she would hold that moment in her memories forever.

The moment, however, did not last. One of the guards behind them coughed, and it suddenly felt as if they were on a stage, playacting the roles of mother and son.

"What have you come to discuss?" Arator asked, his tone reverting to polite, as if she were a stranger instead of his mother.

Well, and why not? She was both.

"I would like to know how my son fares." She looked upon him tenderly, her heart clenching at the thought of him striding headlong into a war they might not win. She gestured ahead. "As we talk, perhaps we could walk the full circle of the city and then wander the bazaar?"

He chuckled and led her onward. "Sometimes I forget that you know this place."

"I know it well indeed—as it once was. I was briefly ranger-captain of Quel'Thalas, if you did not know." Because how could she know what he might have learned of her past?

"Father has told me some things about your history." Arator was choosing his words so carefully, so formally. "Most of all, he speaks of your strength as a leader and your proficiency as a fighter."

"Those are indeed some of the things he values most."

"He—" Arator paused; he was still watching his words. It was difficult for Alleria to stroll so slowly; she was more accustomed to striding everywhere, if not running directly toward danger.

They were in the Walk of Elders now, a busy and well-kept section of the city with a few travelers still finding their way and ogling the glorious architecture. Golden trees swayed overhead, and potted plants floated in small groupings that brought a breezy, carefree feeling to the paths. The scent of roasting meat and fresh bread wafted out of the Wayfarer's Rest inn, and Alleria remembered a delightful mutton stew she had enjoyed there, long ago. With Turalyon. When things had been easier.

"Do you and your father not get along?" she asked gently. "My own relationship with my mother was strained. She wanted me to be something I was not, and I was hotheaded when I was younger. At least we managed to reconcile before . . ." Now Alleria trailed off.

Growing up with Vereesa, surely Arator knew the stories, knew what had become of most of the Windrunner family. She did not need to dig up old graves, not when they had so little time together.

"The war," he finished for her, the words spoken darkly. He shook his head. "No, it is nothing like that, nothing so serious. Father has much to teach me, and his experience with the Light and on the battlefield is invaluable, but . . . How to put it into words? Sometimes I would like to go fishing with Turalyon the man instead of sharpening my sword with Turalyon the High Exarch of the Army of the Light as he scrutinizes my whetstone." When she did not immediately speak, he hurried to add, "I think the world of him, I do. He's my hero. It is just . . ."

"You knew him as the hero before you knew him as your father, and that cannot be reversed so easily."

He nodded with relief. "Exactly so. We have much in common, but I often feel like he sees me more as a project . . . and less as a son."

Up ahead, a family purchased pastries from a vendor's cart. The mother carried an infant strapped to her chest, while the father held the hand of a toddler who chattered excitedly about his favorite flavor. When Alleria looked at her son, it was hard to imagine he had ever been so small and innocent. She had only ever seen him in those years thanks to the Light—and from far, far away. She had never held his sticky hand, did not know what his favorite flavor of tart might be.

"It was so hard," she said roughly, one hand around her emerald necklace. "So hard, putting you in Vereesa's arms. Knowing all the tender moments I would miss. Knowing that if I did not leave, no one would get the chance to experience those moments because the entire world would be a charred husk. You were so tiny. It was the hardest thing I have ever done."

"I know that in what you state you're seeking absolution," Arator said, his voice low. "Aunt Vereesa did well enough in raising me, but she was a poor substitute for what I needed." He looked up at her, curiosity in his eyes. "Though I do not deny when I was alone and sad and sought your comfort, I found you in the Light. It is what brought me to this calling, dedicating myself to its cause."

Arator stopped in front of a crumbling house and turned to her. This place had long ago fallen to the Scourge and was just now being rebuilt; a fresh stack of stone waited beside a half-constructed wall, and someone was nurturing two freshly planted seedlings on either side of a gaping hole that would one day again hold a red-painted door.

A family had lived here, once. They had been driven out—or worse. But now the people of Silvermoon had come together to rebuild it, and soon new memories would be made here.

Broken things can be fixed, Alleria thought as she watched her son's tall, broad-shouldered shadow stretch longer against the wall. If there was hope, there could be healing.

"I prayed you felt it," she admitted. "There were moments when I could see your face through the Light, and my heart ached that I could not hold you as a mother should. There were times it was as if I felt you crying out for me, and I reached out in turn and hoped you knew that you were loved. It is as if there has always been a string from my heart, extending to yours no matter how far away. Everything is connected, like the light with the dark. In perfect balance." She regarded the two serpentine dragons flowing up each of his arms.

"Aunt Vereesa told me something similar once. She said to

never doubt your love and to trust that you would never leave me by choice, but that you were a great hero and that the entire world depended upon you. And I never understood, until one day . . ." His hand became a fist. "You, me, Father. We have a duty, a mission that others don't possess. The first time I was called to war, it was as if I finally began to understand you."

A shadow passed overhead, and Alleria looked up to find a golden dragonhawk streaking across the sky, likely headed to Sunstrider Isle with a traveler on its back. Its shrill screech echoed, and Arator looked up too, shielding his eyes with his hand, and smiled.

"I am happy to be understood," Alleria said, an ache in her throat, "even as I know what your father and I did cannot be fully forgiven . . ."

You are a monster. This boy can never understand you, cannot see you for what you are. Just give in. The Void knows you. The Void welcomes you. Give in. Become what you truly are.

"—but I am grateful for your grace. I hope that one day Azeroth will be safe, and we can spend so much time together that you grow sick of my company."

A rueful chuckle. "Perhaps one day it will be so. Perhaps in another world things would be different. But this is the only world we have, and we are both dedicated to fighting for it, no matter the cost."

A WHISPER OF WARNING

They left the new construction and passed into the Royal Exchange, where gold-inlaid benches were placed at thoughtful intervals and people were queued up outside the auction house and the bank just before closing time, tapping their feet and muttering about the wait.

Alleria's pulse quickened; the sun was going down, and she did not have much time left. They were silent as they entered Farstrider's Square. Here, archers were lined up in neat rows, hitting their targets with absolute precision while nearby a mounted cavalry practiced maneuvers on their hawkstriders, their violet feathers flashing in the dying sun.

"What is it you do when you are not fighting?" Alleria asked.

Arator scratched his scruffy chin. "Like these warriors, I spar with my comrades. I dedicate myself to the study of the Light."

"And do you have . . ." So awkward, to broach the subject. "A special someone?"

He looked away, blushing. "Mother, please. I am a servant. A warrior. What kind of life can I offer another when I am dedicated elsewhere?"

"There is always room for love, my son . . ."

She trailed off, feeling beyond hypocritical.

Thankfully, he did not call her on it. "I have all that I need. I have a life here."

He did. And she knew nothing of it.

You know nothing of him. Why would he listen to you? Love you?
You are nothing to him.

"Or at least," Arator said, "I have a duty here."

He will fight and fail.

Turn him to our cause.

They were in the Court of the Sun now, standing before a grand fountain bedecked with giant fish and graceful sin'dorei, the clear blue water providing a peaceful and musical counterpoint to the tall dignity of Sunfury Spire looming above all. Lor'themar was in that grand palace somewhere, possibly looking down from one of its many cupolas or balconies, waiting for Alleria to over-stay her welcome and meet the wrath of his soldiers.

The moment to delay was over.

"Listen, my son. Something is coming," she said, her voice low as they rounded a bend where the walls were closer and the shadows darker. There was no one nearby just then, but ears were everywhere, and the guards would not be far behind them.

"Khadgar told me there are signs," she continued in a hushed voice. "Portents. The artifact I am chasing heralds some new danger, an enemy lurking in the shadows. A battle is coming, and I must beg you as your mother and as a former ranger-captain of this very kingdom: stay out of the fight."

Arator stopped midstride, his brows drawing down. "You can't be serious."

A WHISPER OF WARNING

He doubts you.

He hates you.

"I have never been one for humor. All I have ever wanted for you was a life of peace, away from the battlefield. That is why I left you with Vereesa. That is why I told you so long ago that war was not glory. Defending Azeroth is my calling. It need not be yours."

The warmth in her son's eyes winked out; he looked every one of his years then, a man grown and hardened in battle. "Listen, Mother. You may not know me as well as you would like, but you must know I would never abandon my duty. I would never shirk my responsibility and leave the risk to my fellow Knights. Can you imagine Father sitting home during a war? What would he do—knit socks and sing songs and pretend the world was good and safe while others died in the streets because he was not there to defend them?" He shook his head and turned away from her, pulling down his sleeves to cover his tattoos again. "Do you think me unworthy?"

Alleria stepped around to face him. "It is because I *know* you are worthy that I urge you not to fight. Live to rebuild this world from what may become of it. Do not fall as I have watched so many fall. There is nothing I fear in all of Azeroth, in any world in any universe, except losing you."

He would not meet her eyes; he was gazing past her, beyond

her, searching himself. "Perhaps . . . I am not yours to lose. When you gave me to Vereesa, you gave up the ownership one soul feels over another. Like you, I belong to the cause, even if it hurts you to hear that."

He will hurt you, again and again.

There is no pain in the Void.

Abandon your flesh.

Become more than this.

"The hurt is worthwhile," Alleria whispered. "It is a gift to see you alive and grown and taking your place in a world being rebuilt from rubble. I cannot agree with your decision—it is not what I had hoped for you, not what I would choose—but I am proud of you, my son."

His eyes briefly closed, and a small smile touched his lips. "It is strange that sometimes I feel closer to you when you are far away, but right now . . . I felt it again. Just like that day in the Valley of Heroes." His golden eyes opened once more, and he ran a hand through his long, sun-burnished hair before continuing onward.

They rounded a corner and stood in the courtyard before the bazaar, where vendors were beginning to close shop for the evening as families hurried past on their way home with full baskets and bags. Nearby, between two archways, stood a statue of Kael'thas Sunstrider. With perfect timing, the guards

"It is because I *know*
you are worthy that I urge you
not to fight. Live to rebuild this
world from what may become of it.
Do not fall as I have watched so many
fall. There is nothing I fear in all of
Azeroth, in any world in any
universe, except losing you."

emerged, reminding Alleria that those who threatened the Sunwell could not feel welcome here for long.

Arator ignored them. He pointed at the sky. "And look. There is Turalyon's Hammer. As if he is calling us home to supper."

Alleria gazed at the constellation, the faint stars just beginning to twinkle in a sky gone indigo. If she did not leave Silvermoon soon, things were going to get uncomfortable. She would prefer not to face Lor'themar again, especially not in front of her son. They had almost reached an understanding, and she did not wish to be scolded and escorted out like some common criminal in front of him.

"He is calling you, perhaps. As my mission calls me. Will you walk me to the gates?"

Arator held out his arm again, and after hesitating for a moment, she took it. The irony amused her. She had been absent during the years he would have needed to hold her hand to learn to walk, and now it was he who led her.

Her baby. Now, this man.

"Are you sure I cannot convince you to stay home? To marry one of the Breezeblossom twins and raise a future baker or tavernkeeper? Someone to carry on the Windrunner name?"

Arator sighed. "Just when we've found common ground . . ."

"Our common ground is fighting. The difference is that I don't have a choice and you do."

A WHISPER OF WARNING

He withdrew his arm with a glare. "I do not, and I am sorry you cannot see it. And *that* is our common ground. Stubbornness. Neither of us has the option to reject our calling, no matter the cost."

They walked, side by side, and Alleria could feel her son's disquiet. She had felt this same weight from Turalyon time and again, after an argument about her communion with the Void. There was a vast chasm between them. If only she could reach them, her men. If only they could accept her for who she truly was—

And, well, that was all that Arator wanted from her, was it not?

"You have the strength to protect your world, so you must fight as I did. But know that I will never want this for you," she said. "A mother will always want to protect her young."

"Your love I have never doubted," he responded sadly. "But I wish I knew you better, and I wish you would stay long enough for us all to grow bored and quarrelsome with each other. I cannot know myself unless I know you."

"Knowing oneself is the work of a lifetime," she admitted. "And I have been working at it for several. Change is part of life, but loving you is my only constant."

Her pace slowed as they neared the gates. The guards waiting there watched her closely, weapons in hand, as the guards behind them fanned out, forming a wall.

"Your love I have
never doubted," he responded
sadly. "But I wish I knew you better,
and I wish you would stay long enough
for us all to grow bored and quarrelsome
with each other. I cannot know
myself unless I know you."

A WHISPER OF WARNING

"Knight Arator," one of the guards said, inclining his head.

Arator returned the gesture as they passed through the gates.

Once outside the city, Alleria felt a wave of relief; she had lived up to her half of the bargain, and now she was again beyond the judgment of anyone within the city walls. She swiftly withdrew her armor from her enchanted bag and was soon sighing in relief to again bear its weight. Her armor, like the whispers of the Void, had become an intrinsic part of her, and she felt more herself with it than without.

Arator, too, could sense the change. "Light bless you, Mother," he said formally with none of his earlier warmth. "May your mission prove fruitful."

"I would prefer its urgency be proven unfounded, but I carry your hopes with me, my son."

She regarded him for a long moment, and he stepped forward. They embraced stiffly, and Alleria remembered what it had felt like, to carry a child within her and dream of meeting the new soul she'd felt stirring for months. She wished she could keep him as safe as that, shield him with her body from all the horrors of the world. But he was taller than she was now, a man of his own making, and he had made his choice. All that was left for her was to support it.

She wished she could have held him forever. "Goodbye, Arator."

He stood back. "May the Light guide you in your quest, Mother."

She knew he was annoyed with her, but she could tell that he was still sorry to see her go.

Arator turned and passed back through the gate, and Alleria watched him with a fond smile. He walked like a warrior, shoulders back, a loose-limbed, athletic elegance to his gait.

He is leaving you. He detests you, hates what you are. He is glad to be rid of you.

Alleria sighed.

This visit could have gone better—but it could have gone worse.

She had doubted he would heed her words, but she had to say her piece. At least now he knew her feelings, feelings she had held inside for years and years, hoping that one day they could speak honestly. They were cut from the same cloth. Just as she had to find the Dark Heart even if it meant leaving her family again, so he had to run into the battle that would follow, even if it meant disappointing his mother.

He will die on the battlefield. He will fall. You have failed him.

This was not the first time Alleria had walked away from her family, and she doubted it would be the last. She could only hope that the next time she stepped through Arator's door, it would be with tidings of victory and an end to whatever evil threatened Azeroth. Perhaps then Lor'themar would welcome

It will never happen. You are changed. You are different. They will never understand you. They do not want to understand you. You do not need them, they do not want you, you must—

"No!" she barked. "That is enough lies for one day. I will have this moment."

her as a hero, and Turalyon would speak his mind, and Arator would settle down with someone nice, and Alleria could sit with her family and have a simple meal with no talk of impending doom.

It will never happen. You are changed. You are different. They will never understand you. They do not want to understand you. You do not need them, they do not want you, you must—

"No!" she barked. "That is enough lies for one day. I will have this moment."

For once, thankfully, the whispers quieted altogether. She knew it would not last, but perhaps the Void understood that on this topic she could not be swayed.

She loved her family, and she wanted what was best for them, and for now that was enough. Perhaps her son did not know her well . . . but he wanted to, and that was something precious.

The city glowed behind her, lit with bright crystals and merry fires, but Alleria Windrunner walked away into the darkness, again, always—and she walked alone. But this time, it was not violence that drove her forward.

It was hope.

THE LILAC AND THE STONE

CATHERYNNE M. VALENTE

Among all the great craggy, unfeeling boulders of our people, Dagran was always my flower.

For all the good it ever did him. Or me.

Few can imagine what it costs a gentle soul to grow up a dwarf. It may even be worse than to come into this world saddled with the soul of a daughter instead of a son. That one singular roll of the bones determined much of my life before my fist first found my mother's braid. My body robbed me blind with its first breath: it was a girl's, and therefore not what my father wanted.

I am Moira Thaurissan, daughter of Magni Bronzebeard and his bride Eimear, princess of Ironforge, widow to the Dark Iron Emperor, mother to his heir Dagran II, and I have been angry since I was old enough to walk the path set before me. Sometimes, I think my anger will outlive me. That they will close up the earth over my body, and long after I am forgotten, some brutal, black hardened jewel left from my rot will work its way up out of the moss, hissing and spitting and still scalding hot. Maybe they will use it to warm a village somewhere. An eternity of cozy hearths and ready stews fueled by this bitter fury I carried but could never fully satisfy. I like the idea of that.

For a long time, I wore my anger on my chest, glinting like one of the gems on that shield they can't stop squabbling over. As if it could shield me, as if it could shield anyone. But in time I learned that anger shown is anger wasted. It only puts others on guard, makes them fearful or defiant, pushes them to dig into defensive positions, fuels rumors of madness and whispers of revolt, and blunts its own edge as even fear fades with overuse. So I learned to make that shield gem inside myself, pushing the rage deep down into the caverns of my heart, compressing it into a crusted geode of pain, all so that my husband's people might like me a bit better. All my mistakes have come from that horrid boiling crushed place inside me. Sometimes . . . I wonder who I might have been without it.

I do not worry that my son will make those mistakes. I worry that he will never get the chance to make them. Because for all that, there *is* power in righteous fury, and poor Dagran does not have even that to protect him. In this great vast universe, that boy has never looked on anything with hate or disgust or fear or rage, only curiosity and longing to understand. He has no fury to keep him safe. He has only me. But all these great officials who gather here to bicker over old jewelry will not suffer me to stand between him and their punishing world forever.

And we welcomed them, despite the ugly expectations they wished to shackle to my son. We welcomed them to Quench-vessel Hall, my late husband's favorite retreat, a vast house built into the great caverns that make a whistling war flute of the subterranean plains that stretch out from Shadowforge City. We welcomed them, and they looked at my child like he was a particularly unimpressive carpet.

Quenchvessel Hall is a pretty place, though too enormous to ever be called a home. Dagran and I both have paced out the rough rock clerestories and walkways, the polished black marble arcades over molten underground rivers connecting one vast wing to another, the silver-silled lancet windows and balconies woolly with firebloom. One could walk for hours, staring out into acre after acre of luminous stalactites and glittering stone, hours upon hours, and never leave the house.

I have always walked to clear my head. To have a moment of quiet without these stomping bellowers demanding to be satisfied every second—and there is never a second in the life of a queen-regent without stomping, unsatisfied bellowers. Sometimes, I think I see my son running ahead of me as he used to do, small and sweet and careless, laughing as I have not heard in many years. Then it is gone, vanished around a blue-agate column into the shadows of my mind, and all that remains is regret—and the problem.

I have gone to several meetings now concerning the great shield discovered by explorers in the Badlands. I have examined the bloody thing closely—and it *was* bloody, splattered with the stuff, blackened and cracked and centuries dry. The battle side was quartered by a cross of three delicately braided metals: iron, bronze, and gold, dividing the massive surface into four images, faded by time and bludgeoned by experience. An ornate and delicate silver crown barnacled in black pearls and jewels of purple and green against a black field, with a great war hammer thrust through its circlet whose pommel was a simple knuckle of plain, rough-hewn granite. An eagle and lion rampant addorsed on a field of white, and below them a branch bearing both orange blossoms and oranges in the mouth of a helpless lamb. A great iron goblet studded with chunks of onyx and amber and filled with blood pricked out in ruby dust. And last, a tower of blackrock, its masonry cracked through the middle, engulfed in flames of topaz and garnet that spilled up and out into the other quarters, threatening them all. And all around these designs, a border of that same braided metal, but with a fourth ribbon of silver on which is engraved runes so ancient not even the most learned scholars dare claim the capacity to read them, or even swear to it that they represent words at all.

I have listened to the evidence and the arguments, both practical and born of passion. I have closely examined the artifact. And I have come to the definitive conclusion that I do not care about that slab of metal and time-chewed leather. It is nothing and means nothing. Artisans with too much time on their hands trying to impress some long-dead king who wouldn't know rampant from passant but I'm certain truly excelled at separating brains from skulls. It's a very finely made and rather expensive reason to fight, nothing more.

Oh, is it for the Bronzebeards because the method of braiding such metals so finely together is a secret of their smiths alone? Is it for the Dark Irons because the rubies and opals and onyxes were cut and finished in their style? Or is it for the Wildhammers because the eagle and the lion together make the gryphon? Do let us consult the heads of all the great families. Perhaps we could have a war about it.

And so on and so forth for the whole long history of dwarvenkind's struggle to stop being piles of rock and start being people. We certainly will get around to finishing the process. Any day now.

It's all a dance, a pretty
pantomime, each step careful,
graceful, precise—even as we
all pretend to be big, brawling
brutes with sword pommels
for brains.

But not today.

Today they argued, then quarreled, then thundered about, puffing up their deltoids like birds in mating season, then various mothers were insulted, and the standard past crimes dredged up, then lunch.

But lunch is never just lunch, oh no. Statecraft is tablecraft, on both sides of the board. I suspected this lot starved themselves for a month before they arrived so that their vigor and appetite would cost the Shadowforge vaults as dearly as possible. It's all a dance, a pretty pantomime, each step careful, graceful, precise—even as we all pretend to be big, brawling brutes with sword pommels for brains. Even as we all know it's going to end up in a museum or a monastery where everyone can look at it but few will ever take the time. It's absolutely *exhausting*.

And I am so much better at it than they are. How could I not be? Not one of these walking belches ever learned to bake their own bread or bothered to scrub their own tables after they slopped ale all over it—and mind you don't spoil the grain with your fat fingers, Grunthin Windwhip, you gryphon's arse flea. Oh, has Thurn Berylbane, the great bat-fart of Ironforge, let the oven get too hot and spoiled the morning loaves? How many times shall the cook beat him?

No times whatsoever. They were born for better things, weren't they? They are so terribly good at pounding on tables with their fists and bellowing demands, while I do the quieter work. It's beneath them to know a favorite meal can make a man more agreeable to a cause, or a luxurious bedroom set with the same flowers his mother once loved can soften his resolve, or sour ale that does not agree with his stomach can turn his temper against everyone equally, or how a silly little sticky latch on a stable might release his ram to mate with one of our ewes and remind him quite vividly of the value of alliances, or how guest gifts given with enough care can put him in debt without his ever even knowing he has agreed upon terms. These proud strutters think the dance of state begins at their arrival. They cannot imagine the music began weeks before, nor fathom the advantage of owning the dancing floor.

Did I try to teach my son these things? Of course I did. It took so long to understand them myself. I resisted all that for years upon years. I didn't *want* to know it. My mother's world. My mother's ideas. My mother's skills and subtleties when I wanted only to become my father: body, soul, mind, and throne. Not only to become as he was, but for him to see it in me, see it for himself—and not because my dying mother told him to look. If I learned to bake the braided bread and spin the thinnest metal into linen thread to make it shine and memorize the leverageable childhood pains of every politically significant man in Khaz Modan, I would still be nothing to him.

It would take years
for me to mold myself into
the leader my people needed. To
bury my anger, to learn the ways of
the Dark Irons, to stop letting my
father's disappointment
steal me from myself.

Magni Bronzebeard would never turn his face to his daughter and see a son.

So many mistakes because I wanted only to be like him. To solve every problem by making it bleed. So much pain because other solutions didn't make me feel like my father's heir. So much ale spilled on so many tables, and for what? It would take years for me to mold myself into the leader my people needed. To bury my anger, to learn the ways of the Dark Irons, to stop letting my father's disappointment steal me from myself. I had made mistakes in the doing of it, but it was I who saw my husband's vision realized, who helped free the Dark Irons from the thumb of Ragnaros. And it was I who allied them to the other clans, who led them into the broader Alliance. And it was only then that my father saw me for what I was and not whom he thought I should be.

And I would never let this be the model for rearing my own son.

Unlike the nobles braying about our table, my boy has baked his own meat pies of boar and bear, spun his own wool, stitched his own tunics, washed the stones of Quenchvessel Hall until they shone and he bled. The trouble has never been that he does not know how to play the game—it's that he refuses to play it at all. He will hole up with his books, pretend not to know these things. He will not behave like a dwarf, only like Dagran, and a flower among slabs of rock must appear to be stone or be crushed.

The high steward Angrid Coldfeast prepared and set out the meal alone. The clan representatives ignored her as she entered. Who was she to them? Just an old woman. Might as well be a piece of broken furniture fit only to rest a mug of beer on, stooping and scuffling on the flagstones, her back cameled with age, eyes distant and glazed, arthritic hands quivering on the lip of a great golden platter stamped with the gryphon sigils of Wildhammer, piled high with sugared morels and spiced haggis, blood sausages smothered in boiling bramblebear butter sauce imported from Kul Tiras. Grunthin was such a greedy, plump little cakesnatch when he was a boy. I never once wanted to hear his mother complain about how he stained his leathers with drips and glops of bramblebear butter sauce, but I am glad of her whining now.

After settling Grunthin and Falstad Wildhammer, poor old doddering Angrid steadied herself as she slid a bronze platter stamped with the seals of Ironforge. The huge plate was crammed to the edge with icefin fillets, honey-spiced lichen, tender boar stuffed with winter figs. Thurn Berylbane licked his chops. Whenever he was ill, his old nurse made him honey-spiced lichen to suck on. It made him feel drowsy and agreeable, cared for and unthreatened. But Thurn had not come alone; none of the clans send only one mouth to argue with. The Bronzebeard representative, my uncle Muradin, reached eagerly for a fistful of arctic char from Dun Morogh, his favorite, preserved out of season.

And then there is my plate: blackened iron, bearing bitter greens, crayfish hearts still in their shells, and a round of red spiced braided bread seeded through with dried fruit, onions, bits of hard cheese, and morsels of bacon, as big as my head and twice as pretty.

I know all this because I planned it. I learned long ago that I detest surprises, though there was one I welcomed gladly: Angrid. Angrid is older than magma. When the emperor and I first came here, young and in love and determined to fill every one of these rooms with a child or at the least exhaust ourselves trying, Angrid was already stark white of braid. As far as I know, she sprang whole from the foundation stones of this place when the first hammer struck the first slab. When we met, she was mistress of the kitchens, a bare spinster branch of a minor family's scrub brush. Now she is the singular gem set in Quenchvessel Hall's stark prongs. Nothing passes here that she does not know. But few who pass here know her, and that is how we two have devised it since I became a widow and she became my spymaster.

Angrid's hand was perfectly steady as she poured hot vinegar into a stone bowl to dredge my crayfish through—because her hand is always perfectly steady, unless I tell her it ought not to be. I make apologies for her infirmity and her hearing trouble when she possesses neither. The great clan leaders do not care. They do not even see her. She is nothing to them.

We devised our finger language when I was a young bride expecting to visit here often—of course, I never got the chance to be an old bride. We became so quick and subtle at it that we would finish our conversation before anyone else thought to ask why I so incessantly played with my signet rings or touched the prongs of my forks or soundlessly tapped my knuckles with my thumb.

Where is my boy? my fingers asked.

Where else? In the library, hers answered.

Still? What is he doing? asked the raise of one eyebrow and a sharp dip of my chin toward the north wing of the house.

Nothing useful. No one ever sired an heir on a book, that's all I know, said the subtle movements of her fingernails on the edge of the plate, then tugging her wispy, snowy mole-spattered muttonchops I have come to love so dearly.

Summon him. He ought to be here.

He will not come, my queen. You know that.

Stubborn like his father. And mine.

And you.

I tossed a heart shell onto the floor and sighed. "Brothers,

I am nearly ready to call for my mace to break this bauble in four pieces. We can each take one home, pitch the last into the sea, and go back to our usual business, which is still warm and waiting for us."

"No one who thinks that would satisfy Ironforge ought to call me brother," Thurn Berylbane snarled. "The shield belongs to us. How can you deny it, a child of the Bronzebeards yourself? Are your loyalties truly so bent to the Dark Iron, when your son reflects the lineage of both houses?"

"Subtle as a cudgel, this one. My first loyalty is, as ever, to our people."

Grunthin snorted around a butter-greased mouthful. "Oh, just let us fight it out, Moira. It's what we're going to do anyway, in the end. I don't know why you're putting it off. This will all be over as soon as I am allowed to make my points *clearly* and *efficiently*." Windwhip held up one massive hand and then the other, by way of illustration. "Arguments without fists are like sentences without punctuation. You might manage it, but why make so much more work for yourself and everyone else? Easier to just do it right the first time."

Falstad looked about to interject but was cut off by Thurn.

"Oh, I heartily agree," the Bronzebeard second slurred over gulps of ale. "Since the start of this council, it's been too long since we've all had it out, either amongst ourselves or with some third party. Give us a fight and more bottles of whatever this stuuuuuff is. More of this. Is there more of this?"

My own uncle looked me in the eye, his beard wet with food I paid for. He cleared his throat as if he meant to say something truly meaningful.

"She won't let it come down to blows. She knows she'll lose," Grunthin cut in, letting it lie there on the table like a new, reeking course no one could be so uncouth as to refuse.

He was waiting for a laugh, a grin, but I indulged him only with a sigh. I know what I am. I know my way in this world. All the careful foods and flowers and codes and whispers will work, but with a dwarf, you will always have to use punctuation too.

As fast as my father ever taught me, I snatched the iron crab prong from its bowl, flipped my grip on the handle, and shoved it hard into the Wildhammer idiot's knee below the table. He screamed in pain.

"Come on, Grunthin," my uncle said. "You set yourself up for that one. I think we all know better by now, hmm?"

I twisted the prong into Grunthin's joint. His eyes bulged. I leaned in close, with the eyes of all those men and their seconds and even the creatures on the shield boring into me, waiting to see which way it would go before choosing a side, the cowards.

"Windwhipped whelp," I hissed. "Did I lose against the

"She won't let it come down
to blows. She knows she'll lose,"
Grunthin cut in, letting it lie there
on the table like a new, reeking
course no one could be so
uncouth as to refuse.

Frostmane, while you huddled in your keep, fearing me more than the trolls who threatened our lands?"

Grunthin would not beg with his mouth. His eyes said it, *clearly* and *efficiently* enough for all to see.

"Go clean yourself up, boy," Muradin said, and you never saw a room empty itself faster—except for my uncle, grinning fatly and smugly across the table.

"Thank you for the assistance, uncle," I said, not without amusement.

"Always happy to clear a bit of room for my niece to maneuver," Muradin acknowledged, inclining his woolly head. "I do hope you're right and these lumps can be soothed by Mummy's soup and Daddy's favorite tune on the lute. But I fear you may not be able to leverage this weight so deftly. They're egging you on, looking to test *Dagran* with all this. They want to see what he'll do, the kind of heir he'll be. They won't go or settle this until he gives them that show." He speared a crab with his own dagger, one with no fancy sigils or jewels, just a hard, sharp, cruel triangle of metal accustomed to use.

"I did all this for my son." I felt my face burn red. "As heir to both thrones, he has the power to steer this council. But, Uncle . . . Uncle, if proving himself to the council, to the powerful families, is only a matter of brute force, you know he'll never be able to pull it off. I am trying to make another way, a way for *him*. Titans know he's not even here to *pretend* he's ready for their sake."

Muradin nodded sadly. "And they know it. They look for him around the doorframes, and every time he is not there, they question more and more whether he ever will be." The old dwarf put his hand on my arm. "I know your father . . . did not do right by you. He broke his promise to Eimear, to look out for you. Keeping someone safe does not mean you deny them the tools they need to make their way after you're gone. But . . . it is not much wiser to protect Dagran so fiercely that he doesn't believe he needs armor at all—or that he will ever walk in that armor alone."

Muradin slapped his knees with his broad hands and stood, adjusting his belt around his belly. The old Bronzebeard warrior glanced at the bloody fork on the floor. "They'll want to reconvene in the morning. Bring him. He's of age. It's beyond time. He's a sweet enough boy, Moira. But he can't rule over dwarves if you won't even let him try to be one."

There is no natural light in Quenchvessel Hall, except in one place. The manor, the grounds, the stables, the armory, even the walls and rivers all sprawl, clatter, rise, and tumble

Muradin nodded sadly.
"And they know it. They look
for him around the doorframes,
and every time he is not there,
they question more and more
whether he ever will be."

deep underground. The stoas and corridors and buttressed colonnades glow a faint red from the hot magma far below, illuminating somewhat every wall and arch, broken by occasional orange flames in faceted lanterns where the shadows grow too deep. Outsiders always found it dreary and oppressive—my people find it safe. Reassuring. Correct.

But there is one place. One place where a new husband, young enough to rip out a strip of the night sky for his wife's shawl if only she wanted it, ordered the craggy stone ceiling breached all the way to the surface, then had it thatched and engineered with clear thick crystal to let in the sun and nothing else. And that single shivering shaft of daylight falls in the portrait hall, on a painting that should not be there, for it shows no Dark Iron ancestor or hero who earned their honor here. It is only a painting of my father, holding my mother's hand gently and looking at her with a private, naked fondness that no paint should ever be able to capture.

There is no path to the great library from the meeting vaults without passing through the portrait hall. It pained me to look on it now, after all that had come to pass. My parents, illuminated by my husband's love because I missed my home, never guessing how short a time I would be wed, and why.

Magni Bronzebeard. My father, who could not let me be or use me well. He held my mother as she died, ripped apart by ice trolls. He stared into the ruin of her guts and swore to be my true father, to be there for me always. And beside those nice words, his only action was to teach me to hit everything in my way as hard as I could.

That is not how my father was taught. I suppose he thought it was, because he enjoyed the hitting parts most, so he remembered them best. But from the moment he drew breath, everyone from the nurses in their veils to the soldiers below in the courtyard believed him to be competently violent and strong. His education was to temper that natural steel with judiciousness, magnanimity, fairness, and the occasional necessary mercy.

With my first breath, my father knew me to be inferior. Weaker, softer, sweeter scented, unserious, ignorable, small. Given a girl to raise to a throne, he deemed her education must be to cut that natural linen into the harshest battle tunic imaginable, because only at her strongest did she stand the slightest chance. I was given no philosophy of rule, no lessons from a foreign mage on the niceties of justice, never taught to hold back if ever I struck a blow to spare the weak or the innocent—a prince who does not use all his strength is still fearsome, even wise and merciful. A princess is merely that: a princess. If she does not swing with every crumb of might, she may never get to swing a second time.

But perhaps that is not fair. Magni thought those things.

Magni arranged my world so. But there are daughters thought not so, and sons as well. Perhaps because my father loomed so colossally in my view I could not see that my pain was only his made flesh, and not every eye in the world was cast against me because I could not be a son. I tried to do better with Dagran, I did try, but I became lost somewhere in it. In the reflections of pain. And in trying to protect him as I was not, I protected myself and left him bare.

Perhaps, when I finally saved myself from this frozen prison of a promise half-kept, when I shone so bright and swung so hard in the depths of a dungeon that the emperor himself raised me up and treated me as his future, loved me enough to let the sun into his stronghold only for me—when I became a queen in my own right, won in the battle of love, which is no less a war than any open plain churned with bodies, that man in the painting took it from me. My own father. He could not bear to let me own my birthright, but neither would he allow me another.

And then my nurse in her veil put this tiny, wrinkled boy into my arms and said: *Make him a king, make him a man, make him a warrior before whom everyone who could not see you for your father's shadow will tremble.*

What was I to do with him? What good could I be to this strange mirror of my Dagran? Another Dagran, but not another. Nothing like his father or his mother, born quiet and gentle and loving as I was not, as no man I ever knew even wanted to be; born so happy and kind that Toothgnasher himself would let him kiss his nose, to whom violence would have to be taught, because he drew only wisdom from my breast.

Oh, my son, my son, what will you be with a mother like me?

The cold sun filtered down through the crystal and lay like a hand against my mother's painted cheek. I watched the light move for a long while. Too long. So many years since I could bear to look up as I passed through the door to the library that inevitably held my son, no matter the hour. So many years since I could stand to look at the family that never was.

On the stone wall behind the painting, a tangled knot of roots, branches, and flowers had broken through the rock. A spring lilac, determined to live, slowly shattering its own foundation as it grew.

But what could it do? Stop growing? None of us can.

And there beyond the grand door and the paintings and the lanterns was Dagran like a seed in its husk. Where Angrid said he would be; where no one ever needed anyone to say he'd always be. In the great library of Quenchvessel Hall, surrounded by books open to chapters and verses and illuminations on a thousand different subjects, reading, as was his preference, nine or so at once, jumping each to each like a butterfly sampling flowers. Dagran Thaurissan II, beautiful

On the stone wall behind the painting, a tangled knot of roots, branches, and flowers had broken through the rock. A spring lilac, determined to live, slowly shattering its own foundation as it grew.

But what could it do? Stop growing? None of us can.

and gentle and quick, hair a fright, fingers covered in ink stains, several seasons from being a man grown, eyes alight with interest and whatever peculiar excitement he took from those pages as from no other source.

On the southern wall, Dagran had hung a length of parchment bearing a detailed, carefully shaded drawing of that damned shield in all its confounding mystery. Half of it was painted in brilliant colors, the precise colors of the real thing. Half was still stark charcoal lines. It really was quite an extraordinary likeness, even the dried blood and dents were perfectly duplicated.

"Did you draw that?" I asked my child.

"What?" Dagran asked, startled as if out of a dream. He groped for a pair of spectacles, a thing I had hardly seen a handful of dwarves come near in all my days, though only the gods know how many of them are half-blind and full-proud enough to need them badly but never admit it. The boy shoved them onto the bridge of his nose under his wild explosion of white hair, long ago fallen loose from its braid. "Oh, that. Of course. Who else?"

"It's very good."

"If you say so. It's not really important."

"How not? All these men have swaggered here strapped with enough weapons to pass for porcupines over the thing. It's what I've come to talk to you about."

"Well, of course it is important, but it isn't *at all*, the shield is just . . . leather and metal. It's nothing dreaming of being something. The drawing of the shield has as much meaning as the shield itself. Both can be true. Do you see?"

When it came to Dagran, I rarely saw.

"How long has it been since you've eaten?"

The heir to two clans hitched up his trousers like a babe not yet grown into them. So thin, so frantic with energy. He waved me off. "I can eat anytime. But I'm so close to figuring it out. It's the words. It's the words I can't get hold of." Dagran flitted from book to book to book, some as wide as my own arms outstretched. "There really isn't a language in Azeroth I don't have a toehold on. Some of the *very* dead ones I might only grasp the basics, but once you know one, the others sort of open up, like a puzzle box. There are only so many ways to put words and symbols together. But I can't nail down a thing about the inscription. The runes don't play well in any tongue I've even heard whispers of. So I thought I might be able to track down that tower. Maybe it's not just a pretty design, but a real fortress that existed somewhere, in some era. Then I thought I might be able to find the artisan who made it. Match the style to those huge heraldic books I used to love—do you remember?"

Of course I remembered. Children always think they are the only ones who remember their childhoods.

"But to do that, I had to understand the style well enough to recognize it elsewhere, and I never cared much for art. So I taught myself to sketch and paint."

"You taught yourself to do that?"

The boy shrugged. "It wasn't that hard. And anyway, it didn't help, so I moved on to something else. There's something about the goblet that bothers me . . ." He scrambled over to yet another huge tome, half forgetting I was there.

"Dagran, I have to talk to you."

"Hmm?"

"Dagran, it's time."

"Hrm. Time. Yes. You know, you're in this one, Mother."

I didn't ask. Nothing in a history book concerning me would be kind. "Dagran. Please. It's *time*. Your time."

He stood up suddenly. All the blood ran out of his dear little face. "Oh," he mumbled. "Oh."

"Muradin won't continue the negotiations without you. They've been counting minutes for you to come of age so they could be rid of me at last."

"I'd rather it keep being you forever," he said quietly and with such defeat in his voice.

"No one gets what they want," I snapped. "Only the scraps from fate's table. Now, you've got to decide, and I cannot do it for you. The easy way or the hard way. Continue as one of three squabbling clans in the council or seize the throne of both your bloodlines and break it. But if you take the latter, you may pay for it in blood."

Dagran frowned. He never showed anger on his face. Most thought he had none of it in him, but I knew. His frown is another man's shriek.

"And how am I to rule? Am I to be like Gran'da?" He turned the page of a tome. "My books say he is the reason Father was slain. Or am I to be like you?" He gestured at an open book. "This says you were cruel. And hasty. And merciless. Is that what you want me to be?"

How should I not be angry?

"Oh, my love. Books . . . they're such unfaithful things. Once you write something down, it's just exactly the same as if it really happened, even if it's not how the day itself went at all. I don't need to read that to know what it thinks of me. They'll tell you I was proud and unyielding, that I ruled with an iron fist. I ask you: What other sort of fist was I meant to use in Khaz Modan? Better yet: What did I do that no king has done before and been called great for it?"

He did not answer. He could not. There was no answer to that. Neither of us spoke for a long while.

"And anyway, I was young. Youth is foolishness, whether great or small."

"And how am I to rule?
Am I to be like Gran'da?" He
turned the page of a tome. "My books
say he is the reason Father was slain.
Or am I to be like you?" He gestured
at an open book. "This says you were
cruel. And hasty. And merciless. Is
that what you want me to be?"

"I am young too," Dagran said quietly.

"As for your grandfather," I continued quickly, "I hated him. For years it's all I thought of, but . . ."

Oh, did I really mean to say it? I did not want to, but you'll do so much for your only child. So much. Even tell the truth.

"But he did the right thing. From his point of view."

Dagran, who never knew his father, snapped his spectacled face toward mine. And there was a flash of fire there after all.

"I don't believe that, and I don't think Gran'da does either."

Tears poured down my face. I did not feel them.

"This may be bitter soil to plant, my son. But it is spring, and you must, or there will be no harvest. The time for learning is over. The time for action has come, and I am so sorry it has. Please believe that if I could take this burden for you, I would. I would have long ago." I sighed and took a last glance at the half-finished painting, so skilled, so wasted. "Look up, when you leave this hall. Above the door. You will see your last lesson. There are flowers that grow on naked stone and thrive. Then report to the meeting hall to address the council, two hours after dawn."

My son straightened his shoulders, just as he had when he was small and running through these halls on a ribbon of laughter and dreams. I knew that proud little spine. He meant to talk back to me.

THE LILAC AND THE STONE

"The time for learning is *never* over."

I sent Angrid to prepare the morning meal and lay it out for the dignitaries to feast on before the council meeting began, hoping full stomachs might soften whatever was to come. She returned far too quickly.

Madam, her fingers said brusquely. *There is nothing for me. It is done.*

Impossible, I replied, already fastening my cloak around my shoulders and pulling on my boots.

But it was not. When I entered the greatroom, I saw a table already groaning, clusters of nobles already loosening their belts to let their bellies breathe. Grunthin Windwhip's knee was bandaged below the board, and he glared at me with one resentful eye. The table was perfect: each dish matched to each lord, each mug of ale carefully watered to fuzz tempers but not reason, and even the cutlery engraved with the seals of each dwarf's house and lineage. And Dagran Thaurissan II stood at the head, where he had been pushed all his life to stand—but he had set his table himself, relying on no servant to do his work.

His fingers flashed briefly against his belt, quick and nimble.

Mother, his fingers said. *Everything's going to be all right.*

I never taught him the signs Angrid and I devised so long

ago. I never taught anyone. He had only watched, for all his life. And learned.

"Honored guests," the child began, and by the time he finished, he would be a child no longer. "You are all fools." The peace of hunger sated vanished in a roar of fury from all assembled. Half a dozen hands went for half a dozen hilts. "You *are* fools." Dagran held up his hands. He did not bellow, he did not roar, he did not strike a blow to cow the rest. But they listened as they never had even when I did all those things. The bastards.

"You are fools, and it is exhausting. I know books are less entertainment than hitting each other because your precious feelings got hurt—"

"*Feelings?*" screeched Grunthin, a bloom of blood appearing on his bandage as his stitches popped free.

"I do apologize, would you prefer *honor*? There's little enough difference."

"Watch your tongue, lad," warned my uncle.

"I have, very well. It is tongues that have troubled me so. That"—he gestured at the inscription on the great ancient shield—"is no tongue recorded by any of the varied races of Azeroth. So why take the time to work it so finely into a shield?"

The gathered officials blinked in confusion.

Dagran smiled patiently. "A shield. What is a shield for?"

THE LILAC AND THE STONE

I confess I quite enjoyed watching these men who spat on me half my life squirm in their chairs like students who had shirked their lessons.

"Grm . . . protecting the guts?" one of the Bronzebeard seconds ventured bravely.

"Yes, and in that capacity, what tends to happen to shields?" Dagran led patiently.

"They get bashed in quite a fair bit," Muradin answered, beginning to catch on.

"Exactly. So why bother with all this fancy nonsense? Why take weeks upon weeks to paint and preserve and embed with jewels, to inscribe runes all the way round and cross the middle, to braid three metals together and filigree them like a lady's bracelet? Just so someone can swing a mace into it and send all those pretty gems flying? I've seen your shields and mine; I've stretched leather and beaten iron to make them. We are practical people. We wouldn't throw away the richness of our mines and the skill of our greatest minds on a shield. A sword, perhaps; parade armor, possibly; a crown, certainly. But a shield is not jewelry. It's a tool. And this is *useless* as a tool."

Doubtful murmurs circled the table. More piles of pies and roast joints and fillets went into nervous gullets.

"Look at it. Every jewel is intact. If this shield ever saw battle, there'd be but empty prongs left."

"But it's got blood on it. And it does bear marks of action," Thurn Berylbane protested.

"Does it?" asked Dagran thoughtfully, as though that had not yet occurred to him. "Is that blood? Or is it paint? Or something even stranger? As for the little wounds on the metal here and there—" Dagran asked Grunthin for his stormhammer, Thurn for a war blade, me for my blade. He held each of them against the damage on the shield. None matched. Then the child who would be emperor pulled a small, delicate hammer and a pair of pincers from his own belt and laid them against the divots.

"The Explorers' League tries to be careful," he chuckled ruefully. "These are the marks of excavation tools. As for the blood, I will come to it in a moment. I have spent weeks in the library researching these sigils and marks, the workmanship of each aspect, the runes themselves, everything. And the answer is: you are all fools."

Don't make them feel stupid, my fingers flashed in warning. *You won't get to finish showing off.*

"This shield was never meant to be used in battle. It is a memorial. It is an apology. And it is a promise. Look again, Wildhammer: there is your gryphon, broken into parts that long to join, tragic, weeping, separate, unable to feast on the lamb alone, no matter how rich. Look again, Dark Iron, there is your fortress, burning beyond salvation. Look again, Bronzebeard, there is your goblet raised in the great halls of Ironforge, filled not with blood but with wine—and all alone, without your comrades to feast alongside you."

Dagran raised his piercing eyes to me. "Look again, Mother. It is not only a crown in the upper quadrant. It is a queen's crown. And thrust through it, a single hammer. Not a war hammer, just a hammer. A hammer to build, not to break. To raise up cities, not to raze them. This shield saw no battle, but was crafted with all this care to tell a story: a story about what happens to our people when we war one with the other. But we came together once. Three metals: iron, bronze, and gold. Dark Iron, Bronzebeard, Wildhammer. We came together to swing our hammers for something greater than shattering bones or filling coffers. Before this Council, before Modimus, before Bronzebeard and Wildhammer and Dark Iron, sometime in the ancient past, our people knew no division. All our clans were one. Under a queen, a queen who had a son with a builder's hands."

Thurn rolled his eyes. "How can you possibly know all that?"

"Because I can read the runes," Dagran said simply. "The trouble of it was the trouble of us: thinking those sigils were all one language, one clan's words, one clan's ideas, one clan's way of being. They are not: they are all three. Each rune is a chimera, a beast formed of the parts of other creatures. Three of

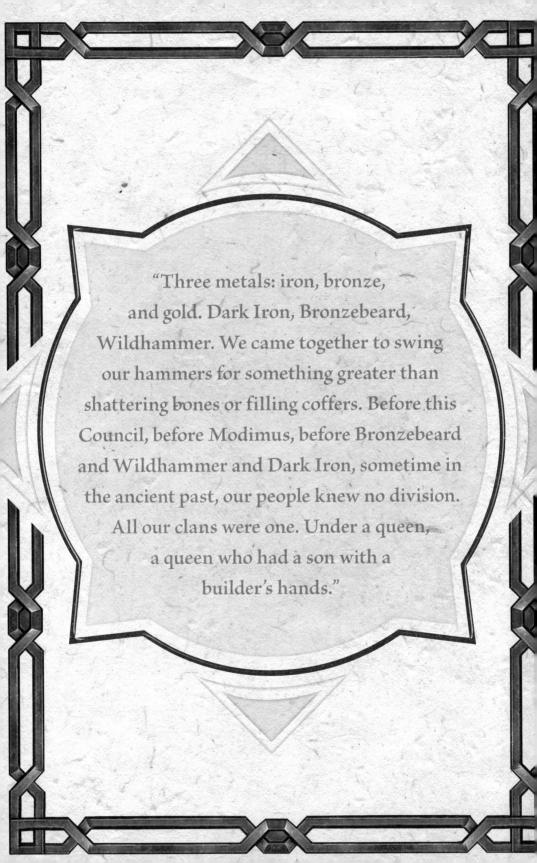

"Three metals: iron, bronze, and gold. Dark Iron, Bronzebeard, Wildhammer. We came together to swing our hammers for something greater than shattering bones or filling coffers. Before this Council, before Modimus, before Bronzebeard and Wildhammer and Dark Iron, sometime in the ancient past, our people knew no division. All our clans were one. Under a queen, a queen who had a son with a builder's hands."

them. The long slash of ancient Wildhammer script here." His quick, clever fingers shaped the characters' anatomies in the air like a painter. "The curt, blunt points of lost Dark Iron runes there; the bold curve of dead Bronzebeard shorthand uniting them. Each letter follows this pattern. I would have seen that much more quickly if the chimera ended there—instead, not only is each letter made of three scripts, but each word is formed from pieces of our most ancient languages, and the sentence itself uses a patchwork syntax: Dark Iron verb conjugation, Wildhammer noun declension, Bronzebeard prepositions and syntactic typology . . ."

Dagran was losing them. He'd become distracted by his own joy of study and puzzles, by the delight of having solved an impossible riddle and the longing to share that, to show it off. My boy had delved far too deep in a mine that had no ore for these men.

Come back, Dagran, I thought desperately. *It is not enough to remember who you are. You must remember who* they *are.*

I opened my mouth to right the course of things, to do as I had always done, to guide and corral and make certain my child did not teeter too thoughtlessly on one of a million steep staircases down to a stone floor.

But I did not. I opened my mouth—and closed it again. I clenched my fingers tight. If he could not right his own course now, with these great men hanging on his words, he never would.

No battle wound has pained me as much as sitting still did then. Never one.

My child stopped. He closed his eyes, cleared his throat. And began again. "And if I am right, they are not just runes. They are a spell. A spell of restoration. If I speak the truth, it will show itself."

Dagran Thaurissan II ran his finger across the inscription on the cross's bar. "We are all fools," he read. Then he ran his finger around the words that rimmed the images. "But fools no further. Fools no further. Fools no further." Over and over again.

The blackened, cracked, dried, and peeling blood shimmered and ran like paint, and in a moment—less than a moment—the shield swam with bright dwarven blood, wet and fresh and hot.

"Will you be fools, then?" Dagran said in a voice I did not even know he possessed. He brought his fist down on the shield with such might it cracked beneath his strength. "Or will you be brothers? If it is the latter, I welcome you. If it is the former, I have no time for your games when there is so much to build."

"Stand in my way or do not," he continued. "It makes no difference to me. Blood speaks true. Those are *our* ancestors. *Our* fathers, *our* mothers, the actual people who lived and died only to become memories, symbols, the seals on your cups and

"Stand in my way or do not,"
he continued. "It makes no difference
to me. Blood speaks true. Those are our
ancestors. Our fathers, our mothers, the
actual people who lived and died only to become
memories, symbols, the seals on your cups and
the food on your plate. They spent untold
fortunes to craft a message that would last
beyond eras, only to tell their foolish
sons that they are family."

the food on your plate. They spent untold fortunes to craft a message that would last beyond eras, only to tell their foolish sons that they are family. If you wish to disrespect their honor, leave this hall and let it be your own affair. I will not. I will stay. I will work. I will build. With whoever is strong enough to hold a *real* hammer."

Dagran tossed the excavation tools on the broken shield and strode out of the room.

Follow me and do not look behind you, his fingers urged.

I did, and in that moment truly thought I could not be more proud of the child I brought into this dark world.

"They will stay," he said beyond the door. "Though I felt more certain in the planning."

"I could not imagine you would do so well," I said quietly. I touched his face, my own baby's face, never to be so young again. "How did you finally solve the runes? You seemed so lost yesterday. You said it was impossible."

Dagran Thaurissan II smiled softly at me. "This place is full of eyes and ears, and only some of them Angrid's."

"I don't understand. It was all so perfect. You found the solution."

THE LILAC AND THE STONE

Ah, there was the boy in him again. Practically wriggling with excitement to tell me how naughty he'd been. "I told you. The shield is nothing. The shield itself, I mean. I told the truth: that thing was never made to be used in battle. It could not have been. It is too fine, too dear—and all those soft metals and jewels make it brittle. Those ancient dwarves made it not to fight, but to speak. Mother, do you understand? To speak to us. Down through the centuries. They knew themselves. They knew each other. They knew, when their fight was over, so their unity would be. They knew it would all happen again, inevitably, again and again. So they made this great object and sent it down the lines of their houses to their great-great-great-grandchildren like a message in a falcon's mouth—and their falcon was time." Dagran laughed dryly, ruefully. "I do get . . . carried away, don't I?"

"Then why not make such a letter easy enough for anyone to read?" I asked. "It makes no sense."

"But it makes every sense! What would you think if you found some bit of scrap metal that said, 'You are stupid'? You'd ignore it flat out and so would everyone else. No, this was the only way to make sure anyone would value it. If it was rich enough, and strange enough, indecipherable enough, then all the clans would have to come together to argue and fight over it, to claim it for their own. And together, perhaps, there might be enough of them that they would have all the pieces needed to comprehend the enormity of what our ancestors were trying to do. What they were trying to *say*. Which is the same thing you and Angrid say with your flowers, your music, your food: *remember who you are, because who you are is what we are.* That shield and that vase of blossoms are the same gesture by another hand. No, it had to be a puzzle. A puzzle so good that no one could comprehend it alone."

Dagran smiled to himself, and in that moment, he looked so much older, so terribly grown. "As are we all, I suppose. Oh, I can't imagine how long it took . . . to plan, to bargain, to spin out gold as fine as thread, hammer out jewels as thin as ice over a winter basin. To devise the gambit. It must have been . . . Mother, I think it must have been someone like me who did it. Who thought it into being and summoned the falcon to fly it into a world he would never know, the light of days on the other side of his own allotted span. Or hers."

I narrowed my eyes. I know my son. I do know him. "And you couldn't help adding your flourish to that lost soul's work, could you?"

Dagran glanced up at me through his lashes with a shine in his eye. "I may have helped a little with the blood spell. Linguistics are quite enough to excite me. I suspected my great uncle and his peers would need something more . . . obvious."

THE LILAC AND THE STONE

I wanted to laugh and whisper and take apart every moment of this victory with him as we used to do when he was small and his only battles were with wooden dwarves and bathtub trolls. Tell him how I had done something not so different in my youth, show him my pride by showing him how alike we are. But I did not. I could not. I did not want to take from his deed by plastering it with my own, making his virtue mine, leaning over him like a shadow he could not escape to find a light he could own.

I can learn. I can.

"I . . . Mother, I knew this day would come, and I knew I would not be ready," he went on. "I had to be better than them. I had to find my own game, because I could never win at theirs, any more than you could. And it will work now. It will. I know it. For a while, at least. It's only ever for a while. Until the need for a falcon comes again." He gripped my shoulders and pressed his forehead against mine. I thought my heart would burst open. "Say you're proud. Say I am your son and you see me, you see in me what was taken from you."

"I see you. My child. My son. I see you," I whispered through my tears.

I was wrong about him. We all were, only they have yet to discover it. He was always my flower, my lilac growing in the most difficult way—but maybe we all are. Flowers beneath the stone. Maybe we all tangle inside. Maybe we scream and charge

He is stronger than
any of us who lived. Even me. I
was never strong enough to stay soft.

And as I watch him turn back to a room he
would own forever the moment he entered, a
room not one single lord had dared to leave, I
became my father at last. Hard as a diamond,
barely able to move for the weight of my
own history, watching the future slip in
between the cracks before anyone
realized it was already here.

and stomp and frown because we know if the armor over our true hearts slips even once, this world will eat our petals whole. After all, the lilac is no less of the earth and earthen than we, no less than the petrified rock on which it must grow. But only Dagran ever stood bare before horrors and told them all he was both at once and would rule them anyway.

He is stronger than any of us who lived. Even me. I was never strong enough to stay soft.

And as I watch him turn back to a room he would own forever the moment he entered, a room not one single lord had dared to leave, I became my father at last. Hard as a diamond, barely able to move for the weight of my own history, watching the future slip in between the cracks before anyone realized it was already here.

THE GOBLIN WAY

ANDREW ROBINSON

ANDREW ROBINSON

M onte Gazlowe sighed, looking out over a vast mining operation from his spot on a platform above the mine's South District floor. This was his fifth "fact-finding" tour of the week, and it seemed like he'd been going nonstop for months, taking stock of less-than-desirable working conditions among the goblins. This one was easily among the worst, though Marin Noggenfogger—Gazlowe's host and guide—acted like everything was aboveboard.

Noggenfogger waved for Gazlowe's attention, looking out of place in a miraculously unsullied all-white suit that practically gleamed amid the smoky air and rancid, dripping space. It was clear he'd recently taken over this operation. "Over here!" he called. Then he turned to one of his bodyguards for help. "Is the two-shift working the . . . uh . . ."

"Longwall shearer?" Gazlowe offered.

Noggenfogger grinned. "Yeah, what you said. The Rock-chomper Three Thousand. Beyootiful piece of machinery, eh?" He beamed more broadly as he gestured down into the enormous mine at a steam-powered behemoth. Its fearsome metal teeth ground relentlessly into the bedrock to get at the vein of iron ore that was the lifeblood of this operation.

"You gotta lean over the railing a little to really get a good look, unless you wanna go down and see it up close," Noggenfogger added, beckoning Gazlowe to the platform.

Gazlowe stepped closer to the railing, waving off his orc bodyguard, Vak'kan. Unlike some goblins—including Noggenfogger, it seemed—Gazlowe had no fear of heights.

As the shearer brought ground ore to the surface, Gazlowe leaned against the railing to watch workers—mostly goblins and some orcs—operate walking mechs with steam shovels, which loaded ore into mine carts, which would take it to a processing plant. A number of workers had bandages wrapped around their limbs, likely because of the discarded machine parts cluttering the footpaths, and a few let out fits of wet, throaty coughs while clamping soiled rags over their mouths.

Noggenfogger gave Gazlowe a fidgety smile, nodding as if to say, "Nice, eh?"

Gazlowe peered back down—and then a section of the railing detached from its mooring with a screech and swung out, leaving nothing but space between Gazlowe and a deadly fall.

He teetered for a moment before regaining his balance—with the help of Vak'kan, who shot out a beefy hand to grab his collar and haul him swiftly backward.

Gazlowe whipped a glare at Noggenfogger, his pointed ears rigid. Had this been Noggenfogger's aim? To stage some sort of accident? As newly installed head of the Bilgewater Cartel and de facto representative of his race to the Horde, Gazlowe was aware he had enemies. But he honestly hadn't thought an attempt on his life would come this soon, let alone be this ham-fisted!

Gazlowe narrowed his eyes. "Look, Noggenfogger, I don't know what ya think ya know about me, but I don't die that easy."

At that, Vak'kan planted himself between Gazlowe and the mine boss, scowling.

"Whoa, whoa, whoa, Trade Prince! Look, it's me, Noggenfogger. I would never do that. In fact, I'm just as shocked as you are!"

For what it was worth, Noggenfogger had gone a deadly shade of pale green—though whether this was from the realization his murderous scheme had failed, or because he was truly taken by surprise, Gazlowe couldn't say. "Believe me," he said, surveying the platform, "that was an *accident*. This cala-mitous breach of construction will not go unpunished, let me assure you!"

Vak'kan took a step toward Noggenfogger, cracking his knuckles with a deep grumble, but Gazlowe put out a hand to stay the orc. He had no reason to trust Noggenfogger—in fact, at this point, he knew that he *couldn't*—but he did see that the head of the Steamwheedle Cartel was at least as unnerved as he was.

Before the tour, Noggenfogger had made it quite clear he hadn't even wanted Gazlowe down there; while flipping through the mine's financial statements, he'd offered Gazlowe more than one drink (and knowing Noggenfogger's reputation for poisons and elixirs, Gazlowe had repeatedly demurred). He'd only be-grudgingly arranged for a brief overview of the operations at Gazlowe's insistence, rambling on about how his time here was limited for the day, what with having a whole other city to run. Ultimately, Gazlowe had used the power of the Horde to strong-arm Noggenfogger into agreeing.

With a practiced eye, Gazlowe ascertained that the platform had been assembled hastily, within the last few days. He ground his teeth together. "This is the problem I keep encountering," he murmured to Vak'kan. "Our people are smart but erratic. Genius ideas, inconsistent execution. We solve difficult

"This is the problem I keep encountering," he murmured to Vak'kan. "Our people are smart but erratic. Genius ideas, inconsistent execution. We solve difficult logistical problems, but all too often it's the fact that we don't pay attention to the details—to quality control—that undoes our best efforts."

logistical problems, but all too often it's the fact that we don't pay attention to the details—to quality control—that undoes our best efforts."

The orc crossed his arms and grunted in agreement.

In the wake of all that had happened since the disappearance of the former "leader" of the Bilgewater Cartel, Jastor Gallywix, Gazlowe had taken pains to inspire the people in his cartel to aim higher and to convince others to do the same. He promoted those who paid attention to detail, who tightened bolts an extra turn and measured twice before they cut. He paid his crew better than anybody else, and the results spoke for themselves. He'd always been known for getting things done, and he'd never disappointed.

He looked over at Noggenfogger. "For now, I'm willin' to believe ya didn't just try to off me. *For now.* So . . . lead on."

Noggenfogger gave a relieved smile. "Smelting and sluicing's up ahead, next juncture."

They walked on toward an opening in the distance, stepping over oily puddles.

"This kinda thing . . ." Gazlowe said, waving one hand to indicate the entirety of the mine. "A lot of the Horde doesn't respect goblins."

Noggenfogger blinked his beady gray eyes.

Gazlowe ducked under a sagging support beam. "Some folks

think we're unreliable"—he pointed back toward the broken railing—"greedy"—he fixed Noggenfogger with a pointed look—"disrespectful. That assessment strike you as accurate?"

Truth be told, those prejudices deeply bothered Gazlowe. But before he could tackle the Horde's opinions, he would first have to change how goblins perceived one another. This mine was a microcosm of a larger problem: rushed jobs, shoddy craftsmanship, poor upkeep, overworking people, and management smiling broadly while siphoning off a fat paycheck.

Noggenfogger barked a bitter laugh. "Like their hands are so clean." He snorted. "Anyways, we hold our own just fine. Most goblins aren't even part of the Horde—or the Alliance, for that matter. They value their independence too much."

As they approached one end of a vast chamber, Noggenfogger began yammering on about how smoothly things were going, praising his own management. "I tell ya, the engineers are always doing . . . engineering stuff. We got explosives guys working explosives. We got drillers, delvers, diggers, and drivers. I started shifts goin' day and night, and nobody leaves till their quota's been filled." He laughed. "Not if they wanna get paid!"

Gazlowe nodded, scoping out the miners. The overseers worked with enthusiasm, shouting threats into bullhorns, but the pace, Gazlowe could see, showed the telltale signs of overwork.

Here and there, diggers stopped to lean on their shovels. Gazlowe, one of the best engineers of his generation, could see indications that the steam-powered ore-shearing machine wasn't operating properly. He could hear a piston misfiring; he could see—and *smell*—the acrid smoke that told him the engine was burning more oil than it should. An audible rattle suggested that the Rockchomper would need repairs sooner rather than later. And he could see the same issues throughout the cavern. The place was full of death machines and . . . more death machines.

Gazlowe picked his way down a slope crumbling with debris and approached a miner transporting ground ore into a cart with a wheelbarrow, not far from a rocket-powered drill sitting idle, dripping some kind of noxious-smelling goop into the dirt.

The worker spilled his haul and swore.

"Hey, pal. Over here! How's it goin'?"

The miner wiped a blackened hand across his sweaty brow and rested on his shovel. "Well, to be honest—" he started, but stopped when he saw Noggenfogger peering down at him.

Noggenfogger wore a carefully neutral face. "Go ahead . . ."

"Splitspark." The miner grimaced. "Sir," he added hurriedly.

"Splitspark. That's right. Tell Mr. Gazlowe how it's goin' down here."

The worker glanced at his overseer, whose stony face was an unmistakable warning. "Uh . . . it's . . . aces! As great as Mr.

Noggenfogger! Couldn't be happier. We're, uh, movin' ore like nobody's business. So . . ." He motioned to the wheelbarrow. "I gotta get back to work. Those quotas ain't gonna fill themselves." He busied himself with collecting his spilled haul.

Gazlowe motioned toward a barrel of water. "Sure you don't wanna rest? A drink?"

Splitspark wiped his perspiring brow, unwittingly showing angry blisters on his hands. "Oh . . . no, I had some water yesterday, thanks."

Noggenfogger smiled and beckoned Gazlowe away. "Y'see? Hunky-dory. Happy miners, happy engineers, happy drivers, happy drill bits. Happy customers. And my operation is clean!"

Gazlowe glanced at Vak'kan, who'd just blown a loud snort of offense and disgust. "Look, Foggy—"

"Noggenfogger—"

"Yeah, whatever."

"*Whatever*?! Now that's a goblin bein' disrespectful. You seem to be forgettin' I'm leader of the Steamwheedle Cartel, *Gazzy*."

Gazlowe cackled. "And *you* seem to be forgettin' that I'm Trade Prince of the Bilgewater Cartel. So, lyin' to my face—is that really how you want to start this relationship?"

Noggenfogger sputtered and his bodyguards started to unsheathe truncheons, but Noggenfogger waved them to halt. "Well, that's about as much time as I got for today," he said.

Gazlowe climbed back up the hill of debris to join him. "What say we keep going?"

Noggenfogger bristled for a moment. *"With respect,"* he growled, "I didn't think you'd be here for so long—and I got meetings and whatnot to tend to in Gadgetzan, so—"

"We're doin' this," Gazlowe assured him with a smile, gesturing for him to continue leading the way. *"With respect*, I'm sure you wouldn't let Gadgetzan get this bad, wouldja?"

Noggenfogger mumbled and guided Gazlowe farther into the mine, their bodyguards trailing them from a distance.

"I know what you're tryin' to sell me here and I'm not buyin' it," Gazlowe said, climbing over a collapsed pipe. "What I'm seein' is your people are overworked and underpaid. Your engineers and tinkers ain't motivated. Your machines ain't gettin' maintained properly. And that's dangerous."

Noggenfogger started to object.

Gazlowe raised a finger, then pointed back to where they'd left the shearing machine. "I can hear the bolts rattlin' on that Rockchomper. So, the most generous interpretation here is that this guy's great with elixirs and potions and whatnot, and he's even used to mayorin', but maybe he doesn't know anything about mining, and a little bit too much about the bottom line."

Noggenfogger snorted. "The bottom line is king! Nobody cares about *maintenance*. They care about *results!*"

Gazlowe grabbed the hand of the nearest worker, revealing the same angry, bandaged wounds he'd seen on Splitspark. "Skipping maintenance impacts results—with your people as much as your machines. How can you expect your engineers to grip a wrench with hands like these?"

"Sure, we get a lotta workers callin' out sick, but that's any job," Noggenfogger countered.

Gazlowe sniffed deeply and felt the rank rasp of oily fumes in his nostrils. "And the air? You *know* it ain't good. You're usin' cheap fuel and rancid oil. You gotta burn cleaner, get the ventilation systems up. And to try and pass this off as a clean outfit? Come on, Foggenniffler."

"Noggenfogger. Marin Noggenfogger." Noggenfogger glared. "And it ain't a lie. I'm clean! Most of that stuff doesn't rise to my level of oversight, so I got plausible deniability of all that mess."

Gazlowe glared back. "That ain't what runnin' a *clean* operation means! *Clean* means you're not pollutin'!"

Noggenfogger's eyes went wide, and he hastened to smooth down his pure-white suit, which had become increasingly wrinkled and stained with greasy droplets. "Oh. Well, then no. The work gives off a natural . . . vapor. What am I supposed to do about that? That's what you call a misunderstanding of frankly confusing terminology."

Gazlowe gestured for Noggenfogger to cross a creaky

"So, the most generous interpretation here is that this guy's great with elixirs and potions and whatnot, and he's even used to mayorin', but maybe he doesn't know anything about mining, and a little bit too much about the bottom line."

Noggenfogger snorted. "The bottom line is king! Nobody cares about *maintenance*. They care about *results!*"

catwalk first. Noggenfogger hesitated far too long before obliging, then Gazlowe followed.

"This ain't just about your bottom line. There's more work we could all have from the Horde—maybe more folks too, if we can run a tighter outfit together. But how am I supposed to talk to a shaman or a druid with your mine belching out this smog? How can we convince clients you're reliable when you got workers out every day with injuries like that?"

"Look, you come in here, you got no idea what I've had to do to get to where I am. You think it's easy schemin' your way into a mayorship? Or the top slot in Steamwheedle? The palms I greased? The elixirs I concocted?"

Gazlowe laughed. "That don't make you special. I rose through the Steamwheedle system just like you. Besides, your rivals and enemies seem to mysteriously go toes-up a lot more than the average."

"Allegedly," Noggenfogger corrected.

Gazlowe cocked an eyebrow. "Seriously?"

"Okay, sure, I may be the best alchemist there is," Noggenfogger backpedaled, "and I got my famous elixir and the occasional pois—I mean, other stuff. But that ain't the point! I had to compete with the likes of Gallywix and the Venture Company, and now I'm the boss here, so I should get to call the shots! Me—and a lotta other goblins—believe that if

I don't take things this far, I'll be replaced—or worse! Besides, I didn't see anyone makin' *Gallywix* clean up *his* act. No one stops the Venture Company. But *I'm* the bad guy?"

Gazlowe paused. "I know you know what happened to Gallywix."

"I know he had to split. But he's got nothin' to do with Steamwheedle *or* this mine."

"You had occasion to deal with him, runnin' Gadgetzan?"

"Yeah, he was a bastard. I hated his guts—but I respected how he did business."

"Did you? Did you respect how he took advantage of his own people and put 'em to work in his mines, after taking everything they owned in exchange for transport away from Mount Kajaro when it was erupting during the Cataclysm?"

"I mean, yeah, harsh. But that's dedication to profit."

"That what's goin' on here? Allow me to explain somethin'. Havin' injured and sick workers using poorly maintained machinery eats into the bottom line. It's short-term gain for long-term loss. Fixin' your tools now, havin' happy, healthy employees now, is an investment—and a damn good one."

"This ain't how we've always done it. Gallywix—"

"Wasn't a businessman; he was a con man and a criminal. Profit above everything else *ain't* good business. A *lot* of people wanted him gone. His own *mother* tried to assassinate him!

THE GOBLIN WAY

Twice! He solved a lot of problems, but he made worse ones out of them. He got stuff done, but he wrecked more. I asked him once if it bothered him, taking advantage of those refugees and working his own people to the bone. Y'know what he said? *It's the goblin way! Supply and demand! Deal with it!*"

Noggenfogger shrugged. "That *is* the goblin way, right?"

"No, it ain't. That was *Gallywix's* way. The goblin way is invention, innovation, partnership. Those things cost a lot, but they earn a lot for every goblin, not just a few," Gazlowe said. "I swear you're missin' my point on purpose. Supply and demand is one way to do things. But we can't only be thinkin' of just ourselves no more. The world is changing."

"There's nothin' wrong with how I run this mine," Noggenfogger protested. "Maybe it's no day at the spa, but production is up ever since I took over."

Noggenfogger's attitude put Gazlowe in mind of another goblin leader he had hoped to forget, because his legacy was as bad in its own way as Gallywix's. Notorious all over Azeroth for their lumber and mining operations. Which was to say, clear-cutting forests and strip-mining areas, leaving barren scars across the land. And the way they operated their oil rigs was reckless at best. Not to mention their arms-dealing with groups that neither Horde nor Alliance found palatable.

"Heard of Mogul Razdunk?" Gazlowe inquired.

"Of course. Former head of the Venture Company. We modeled this operation on theirs."

Of course you did, Gazlowe thought. "Razdunk was aggressive," he said, "but again, he didn't consider the repercussions of his actions, and it caught up to him. He oversaw the Venture Company through expansion in Mulgore, the Stonetalon Mountains, Kul Tiras, Grizzly Hills, Sholazar Basin, and Stranglethorn. But here's the thing. Everywhere they go for a quick buck, it pisses people off, and folks find a way to fight back, to make it harder and harder for them to do business. Pretty soon, everyone there's attackin' 'em. But they just keep doin' it."

Noggenfogger looked less certain. "That's the market though, right? Business is business."

Gazlowe shook his head. "Business is *personal*. When you wreck someone's home, that's personal—and it's bad for business."

They had arrived at a sluicetown—a collection of tin shacks that stood hard up against the sluices that ran already-dirty water over the crushed rock to create a slurry that would separate ore from waste. The ore was run to a massive smelting plant, which melted the rock and purified the ore into metal. This was even worse than Gazlowe had expected. The dim lights flickered badly; the air was oily and stale. His eyes burned a little.

"This ain't how we've always done it. Gallywix—"

"Wasn't a businessman; he was a con man and a criminal. Profit above everything else *ain't* good business. A *lot* of people wanted him gone. His own *mother* tried to assassinate him! Twice! He solved a lot of problems, but he made worse ones out of them."

Gazlowe wheezed. "You gotta get this place ventilated! The air—you gotta know this ain't sustainable."

"Sustainable?" Noggenfogger scoffed. "What are you now, a shaman?"

Gazlowe shrugged. "I've been called worse by better people. But I'm glad you mentioned it. Part of why I'm here is that the elements themselves have taken offense to stuff like what's happenin' here, and what the Venture Company does. I'm hearin' Azeroth is about out of patience with us, and you— mayor of Gadgetzan, leader of the Steamwheedle Cartel—and yeah, head of this operation—you gotta take your share of responsibility for that."

Noggenfogger harrumphed.

Gazlowe had seen enough. He gestured, and Noggenfogger led them back into the shearing cavern, where Gazlowe called out to a goblin working a machine.

"Hey, pal! How many times has that machine broke down?"

"This week? Five," he replied plainly.

"And how much production time has that cost you?"

The goblin resignedly turned his palms skyward.

Gazlowe turned his ire back onto Noggenfogger. "And exactly how many sick days have your *employees* taken because of injury, poor conditions?"

Noggenfogger hesitated. "Well . . ."

"You know about as much about your operation as Razdunk did. He thought he was gonna get rich and become a Trade Prince. What he got was blown up by Gallywix. Don't worship these jokers," Gazlowe said. "Don't model yourself on them. There are better models. Look at the Horde Council."

Noggenfogger scowled. "How'd you get on the Horde Council anyway, eh? What makes you so special?"

"Nothin'. The difference between me and other Trade Princes is I don't think the world is just here to feed me. I learned a while back, you do better when you don't make it all about you."

Noggenfogger looked put-upon. "So, what—you arrive, tell me what I'm doin' wrong, and then throw me to the wolves to fix it? I get the short end, and you go enjoy tea and crumpets?"

"Meh. I don't much like crumpets. Look, I know we got a steep uphill climb, but if we don't change our business—and I mean for all of us—all the goblins, not the mine, we're gonna get left behind. We need to start liftin' each other up instead of seein' each other as competition. And I'm hopin' that you and I can start together."

Noggenfogger took a step back. His beady eyes went wide, and then he scowled again, suspicion written all over his sallow face. "Now it makes sense! It's not enough you got the Bilgewater under your thumb, and probably still some of

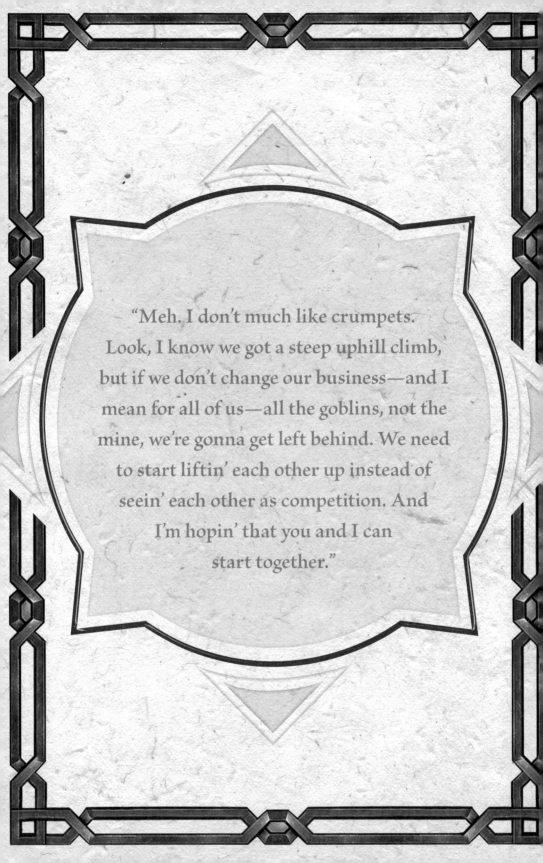

"Meh. I don't much like crumpets. Look, I know we got a steep uphill climb, but if we don't change our business—and I mean for all of us—all the goblins, not the mine, we're gonna get left behind. We need to start liftin' each other up instead of seein' each other as competition. And I'm hopin' that you and I can start together."

Steamwheedle, *and* your pals in the Horde to back your play. You want my little mining operation for yourself! I ask for help, you move in and take over! You're as bad as Gallywix. In fact, you're *worse*! At least he was *honest* about how downright foul he was!"

Gazlowe sighed, pinching the bridge of his long nose. "I don't want the mine. I didn't wanna be head of the Bilgewater Cartel. I didn't wanna have to represent all goblins to the Horde! I mean, between you and me, that's a lotta pressure." He gazed at the whirring shearer wistfully. "I could just be watchin' speed-barge races," he mused.

"Then why'd you take it? There are plenty of goblins who'd kill your whole family for either of those. I'm probably one of 'em."

Gazlowe looked sharply at Noggenfogger, but the mine leader didn't care.

"And you got 'em both," Noggenfogger concluded.

"Some smart guy once said, 'If somebody really wants to be the boss of everything, under no circumstances should they be allowed to have the job.'" He stared fixedly at Noggenfogger.

Noggenfogger looked abashed. "Because they're only in it for themselves."

Gazlowe smiled. "He *can* be taught."

Noggenfogger snorted. "You can't tell me you don't enjoy all that power."

"Oh, make no mistake, being powerful is better than being

powerless. If I wanted to be bigger than Gallywix, I could have that. I'm honestly not interested. But like I said, it's more about the responsibility. The other reason is, you want somethin' done, you ask a busy person."

"What's that supposed to mean?"

"The council chose me because they knew I get things done. Plus," Gazlowe added, "they know I'm a goblin of my word—and loyal to the Horde."

"Big deal. I've got loyal friends in the Horde."

"We both know *that* ain't true. Even I was sellin' to both sides for a while, and there's plenty of goblins who just think gold is gold."

Noggenfogger smirked. "Well, you can't spend honor, can you?"

Gazlowe heaved a sigh.

Noggenfogger furrowed his brow. "Look, what you're saying is great, but how I run things here . . . it's just how it's done."

As if on cue, the sound of mechanical grinding filled the air, followed by an explosion. And plenty of shouting. The huge shearing machine's engine was venting steam, and workers carried injured operators to safety.

Noggenfogger swore, deliberately avoiding Gazlowe's gaze. "This is gonna hold up production. Hey!" he screamed at the workers. "Back to work! And somebody fix that!"

THE GOBLIN WAY

Tinkers and engineers gathered around the machine, which continued to smoke.

"Head machinist's out injured," one worker shouted.

Two other workers lifted blunted and broken tools, exchanging looks of defeat.

Noggenfogger looked on, helpless.

"Whatever else you might be, Noggy," Gazlowe urged, "you ain't dense. I think you maybe could turn this place around, and I can *help* you. But you gotta be willing to play nice, and not just with me."

Noggenfogger looked unmoored. "Our whole system is built on competition, not cooperation. It's how we solve problems. Survival of the fittest, the cleverest, the most ruthless, the best dealmakers. It's how we innovate! Why're you tryin' to fix what ain't broken?"

"Oh, it's broken, and I'm going to show you why. This ain't the goblin way."

They headed closer to the blast radius. The bodyguards joined them. As they approached the drilling site, the workers saw them coming and gave way to clear a path. Gazlowe could hear murmurs, and knew the workers were confused that he was there. Heck, they were confused that Noggenfogger was in attendance, if not there to threaten them.

Gazlowe approached several engineers gathered around the

open hood of the engine, and Noggenfogger followed. "Alright, what's goin' on?"

An older goblin in grease-stained overalls glared. "Don't get'cher pantaloons in a twi—" He stopped when he realized to whom he was talking. "Oh. Mr. Noggenfogger, sorry. Uh . . . look, this beast is long in the tooth. We been washin' out filters instead of replacin' 'em, it's gunked up, the vibrations take a toll. I mean, we been tightenin' bolts left and right, but eventually the threads get stripped, and they just won't hold, the gaskets are kinda shot, and the differential keeps slippin'."

"This machine alone's gonna take a fortune to fix. I can't afford to have this offline for long," Noggenfogger told Gazlowe. "My clients expect shipments on the regular. This'll put me behind."

"If you let me take some of that heat, will you put the work in here?" Gazlowe asked.

Noggenfogger looked grim, but there were no better options before him. "I'll give it a shot."

Gazlowe took a step toward the machine. "Tinker, right? What's your name?"

"Ollie Spracknozzle. You . . . you're Mr. Gazlowe."

"Call me Monte. Yeah, Spracknozzle. You know Skaggit? Used to be head of the tinkers' union here? He's one of my crew. Think he's mentioned you more than once in the positive, Ollie."

Spracknozzle cracked a grin. "He's good people." Then he looked hesitant. "Look, 'scuse my asking, but . . . what are you *doin'* here?"

"We"—Gazlowe gestured to himself and Noggenfogger— "are here to help."

Ollie screwed up his face. "Uh, no offense, but this is a mechanics thing, not a . . ." he paused, clearly seeking a word that wouldn't offend. "Big-shot thing. Bosses don't help. They boss."

Gazlowe grinned. "Let's see if we can change that particular perception."

Noggenfogger was at least savvy enough to grimace noncommittally, so as not to actively antagonize the crowd. His bodyguards and the miners were both on edge.

Still, Gazlowe continued. "As it turns out, Ollie, I happen to be a fair engineer myself. Mind showin' us the problem?"

The tinker hesitated, clearly not used to deference from bosses, then shrugged, motioning one hand toward the engine.

At that, Gazlowe removed his jacket and rolled up his sleeves. He gestured to Spracknozzle's tool belt. "I didn't bring my own, Ollie. You mind?"

"What . . . what are you doing?" Noggenfogger hissed, pulling Gazlowe aside.

Gazlowe stooped beside the broken machine. "What's it look like? Fixin' this thing."

"You're gonna make me look bad."

"Well, hell, Noggenfogger. You say you're a good leader and hustler, so hustle. Get your people in here to help." Gazlowe paused, an idea taking shape. "In fact, yeah. One of them elixirs of yours, it literally makes people tiny—among other things. Break out whatever stash you got, give it to your tinkers and engineers, and actually get them in there to help me fix it!"

Noggenfogger gaped. "Sorry—*give* it to them? For *free?*" he hissed under his breath. "The ingredients alone—"

"Big. Picture." Gazlowe glared at the mine leader, who gritted his teeth, wrestling with the idea.

"Fffffine." Noggenfogger stomped off.

In the next half hour, Noggenfogger (somewhat reluctantly) returned with a case of his special elixir and gave it to a platoon of (somewhat reluctant) machinists, engineers, and tinkers, who had volunteered to help Gazlowe fix the Rockchomper. They got to work.

Gazlowe was in his element now; under the hood solving a mechanical issue, oblivious to the growing crowd of workers trying to figure out what was going on.

Noggenfogger looked on, tapping his foot, glancing around. He moved alongside Ollie. "Spracknozzle . . . the workers who got hurt—how many?"

"Four, Mr. Noggenfogger."

"What . . . what are you doing?" Noggenfogger hissed, pulling Gazlowe aside.

Gazlowe stooped beside the broken machine. "What's it look like? Fixin' this thing."

"You're gonna make me look bad."

"Well, hell, Noggenfogger. You say you're a good leader and hustler, so hustle. Get your people in here to help."

"Tell them . . ." Noggenfogger winced, "that, with no admission of culpability, mind you, I'm gonna take care of them. Like medically, I mean. I've got somethin' to make 'em right."

Ollie looked at Noggenfogger as if he'd spoken gibberish. He opened his mouth to respond but had trouble finding words. "I . . . you . . . that's . . . that'll be a load off their minds."

Noggenfogger nodded.

A gap-toothed grin spread across Ollie's face. "I'll let 'em know, sir!"

Noggenfogger took a deep breath, then addressed the crowd. "This may take a while, but don't worry. We'll get this fixed as soon as possible. So, you all, uh, take the rest of the day off." The workers didn't quite know how to respond. "With pay," he said with a sigh, and the crowd cheered—even as most of them stayed; there was entertainment value to what was happening now.

Gazlowe, working on the engine, smiled in the darkness of the machine's underbelly. His plan had worked. "Hey, Noggenfogger," he called out, "you want to see how to fix one of these things?"

Noggenfogger stooped beside him. "Yeah," he said, peering into the open engine compartment where the tinkers were gathered around Gazlowe. "I'd appreciate it."

Gazlowe grinned. Maybe this was going to work even better than he'd thought.

THE GOBLIN WAY

After his team added a greasy solution of one thing, replaced a few stripped gears and cracked bolts and gaskets, as well as doing some preventative maintenance, Gazlowe turned the final screw, stood, and wiped his hands on his pants. "That should do it." He nodded, and a machinist pulled a lever.

The machine began to rumble and putter before it let out a healthy whir.

Noggenfogger let out a sigh of relief. The workers looked on in a bit of shock and surprise, while those who had helped out from the inside congratulated each other—once the elixir wore off and they regained their size.

Noggenfogger's bottom lip puckered out as he regarded the empty case of his famous elixir, then he studied Gazlowe warily. "You're . . . serious. You want to help. Not take over."

Gazlowe nodded. "Knew you weren't dense. Though you may want to reconsider wearing white when making your rounds next time."

Noggenfogger sagged a bit. "Okay, I'll admit, I could use the help. But you know how tough it is to change things. Could I pay my people more? Some, I guess."

At that, a few workers within earshot gave him reproachful looks.

"Healthcare? I don't even know what that looks like, but we could find a place for a clinic or something. Maintenance, I get.

But I don't have enough tinkers as it is, and the ones I got ain't worth a bucket of warm spit."

A tinker behind him scowled, mumbling a profanity before stalking off.

Gazlowe shrugged. "Or they're feeling misused and therefore not giving you their best."

"And maybe you don't remember what this is like, Mr. Horde Councilor," Noggenfogger said, "but I got people around me— people who don't like profit margins getting eaten into. If I can't produce, they'll find someone who can. Can you help with *that*? Besides, if word gets out that I'm goin' soft, what happens then?"

"Then you got an opportunity to show 'em what's what."

Noggenfogger's nostrils flared. "I'm serious, Gazlowe. You *know* what I'm talkin' about. Other cartels, other Trade Princes are always just lookin' for a sign of weakness to pounce—and you know they'd see me doin' all that—costin' us money—and go in for the kill!"

Gazlowe took that in. "Okay, you may have a point there."

"Damn straight I do."

"What if Steamwheedle had Bilgewater backing your play, takin' a little heat off you? The two biggest cartels working together? Then you'd be workin' from a position of strength."

Noggenfogger weighed the offer—weighed his trust.

"In the meantime," Gazlowe added, "maybe you could put that big alchemy brain to work on . . . the *opposite* of a poison."

"What, an antidote?"

Gazlowe snorted. "No, genius. Cures for diseases. Health potions. Medicines."

"Oh, right. Well, I already got some things in the works. You weren't thinkin' for free, were you?"

Gazlowe crossed his arms. "Sure was. But I'd consider it more an investment than a giveaway."

Noggenfogger cursed under his breath. "Lotta work . . . but yeah. Fine." His eyes lit up. "Plus, it's a whole new revenue stream! Ha! Let 'em call me soft then!" He looked at Gazlowe. "You don't want commission on that, do you . . . ?"

Gazlowe chuckled. "I'll give you that one for free."

Noggenfogger nodded, now grateful. "I guess I . . . appreciate you comin' down here after all."

Gazlowe regarded Noggenfogger. "Humility is a rare quality in a goblin. Especially in a boss. Tells me you're not a lost cause."

Noggenfogger squinted. "I'm not sure whether you just complimented me or insulted me."

Gazlowe smacked his lips. "What about that drink? While you show me the *real* books."

Noggenfogger winced. "You saw through that one, eh?"

Gazlowe sipped from his glass of Badlands Bourbon in Noggenfogger's well-appointed office, which overlooked the mining operations like an aerie. Noggenfogger had opened the ledgers—the real ones this time, he assured Gazlowe— and it was pretty much as Gazlowe had suspected. Grafting, insufficient reinvestment, and skimming from the workers. Standard operating procedure for goblin bigwigs for as long as Gallywix had held the reins. In fact, it wasn't just Noggenfogger taking a bite out of the profits—other bosses were as well, meaning it could be dangerous for Noggenfogger to rock the boat. If so, he could lose more than money by making it stop.

"I see room for improvement."

"You see how much I'd need to do?" Noggenfogger leaned back in his armchair. "Even if I play it totally straight, upgrading the machinery, putting all those safety regs in place, healthcare, paying folks more, I'm gonna be in the red in no time. Rebuilding this place? It's gonna cost a fortune, and it's not just my profits that'll be affected. Maybe things are different in the Horde, but the other goblins, even Trade Princes, have others tryin' to get their cut, and everyone who gets a cut will be looking to get things back to the old way."

Gazlowe sipped his drink. "Like I said, I got a reputation as someone who gets things done where the Horde is concerned."

Noggenfogger rapped his long nails on the wood desk. "Thought you sold to both sides."

"At a certain point, I realized that while gold might spend the same, what happened with the things the gold bought didn't always feel right. Somethin' changed in me after Garrosh was defeated, and I got summoned to repair the damage he left behind in Orgrimmar. You been?"

Noggenfogger shook his head.

Gazlowe continued. "I was chief engineer there for a while before I started up Ratchet for Steamwheedle. Thrall himself asked me to survey the damage. You've met Thrall, right?"

"Thrall the Warchief?"

"He's not Warchief no more."

Noggenfogger grimaced. "I've seen him from a distance once or twice."

"The guy's larger than life. Not that I'd ever tell him this, but I was still a little in awe. I've seen plenty of leaders who ruled by violence and fear. Or by outmaneuvering their opponents and their friends. Seen leaders who ruled through moral arm-twisting. But Thrall . . . he's different. He's . . . decent."

Noggenfogger cocked a skeptical, bushy eyebrow. "I mean, not for nothin', but he named the city after his best friend. He named the *continent* after his *dad*."

"At a certain point,
I realized that while gold
might spend the same, what
happened with the things
the gold bought didn't
always feel right."

Gazlowe considered that. "Okay, fair point. But they had to name things *something*. Anyway, Thrall could have been Warchief as long as he wanted. He coulda ruled the Horde, and maybe the world. But he never seemed to want it. And he's so . . . *earnest*."

Noggenfogger gestured impatiently. "So, he brought you in, gave you the five-copper tour . . ."

"And the place was a mess. But between all that destruction, I noticed Thrall greeting people by name. Hundreds of people. Somehow, he knew the names of folks so far beneath his station that they shoulda been invisible. The big guy just radiated . . . compassion? Empathy? Whatever it was, I'd never encountered it from anyone before. And everywhere he went, these people who'd had their homes, their lives, everything destroyed—they trusted him to help set it right. That trust . . . it was something I didn't see enough of between our people."

"We finish the tour—the Drag, the bank, the Valley of Strength, a zeppelin tower—and he asks me how much it'll cost to rebuild it all—better than it was," Gazlowe concluded. "Now, I realize he's in a bind, and he came to me because, well, I'm the best. Plus, I've helped out before. He trusts me."

"You had him over a barrel."

"That's one way to look at it. Thing is, the way I want to do it—mixing materials, building stronger and whatnot—means more labor, more machines, higher shipping costs, and so on. And I gotta make a profit too; I got mouths to feed. So, I give Thrall my bid for the gig. You shoulda seen his face."

"Didn't go for it?"

"He was . . . set back on his heels. Hard. But I explained what needed done, and he agreed to convince the Horde."

Noggenfogger flashed his teeth. "Heh. Sucker."

"The point"—Gazlowe rubbed his forehead, frustrated—"is he treated me as an expert, a master of my craft. I named the figure, and even though he was unhappy about it, he didn't haggle or argue me down. He showed me *respect*. The leader of the whole freakin' Horde."

"I guess that's hard to come by."

"It is exceedingly rare, my friend, and hard-earned."

"But you and your crew at least gave 'em their money's worth."

Gazlowe gazed at Noggenfogger, who now seemed even more receptive to the message he needed to convey than he had seemed earlier. "I'm gonna tell you somethin' I've never told anyone before," he said, leaning in.

Noggenfogger leaned in as well.

"This is where big-picture thinkin' comes in," Gazlowe explained. "Since he showed me respect, he made me want to earn *his* respect. What I understood at that moment was, Thrall would do anything for his people. And I was gonna do everything in my power to make sure that my people did the best work we'd ever done. That's what he does; you get to know him, and he makes you want to live up to his standards."

"Unlike Gallywix."

"Well, like I said, Gallywix was a sociopath. He offered to do it cheaper, but no. Thrall came to me."

"So, what'd you do?"

Gazlowe made Noggenfogger wait for it. "I dropped my price for him."

Noggenfogger stared, then shook his head. Gazlowe chuckled. "You shoulda seen his face *then*. Like it didn't compute that a goblin's first, last, and only thought wasn't just filthy lucre."

"You tellin' me you didn't make bank on that job?"

"Oh, I made a profit. Just not as much as I could've. Point is, it made the Warchief respect me *more*—and I assume he didn't keep it to himself. I'm hopin' it was the first step to changin' how everyone else in the Horde sees us—and maybe how we start lookin' at ourselves."

He pointed down at the repaired shearing machine. "That accident down there? There was an accident when we were rebuilding too. Folks from all the races of the Horde pitched in to help and get things back on track. Everyone and everything was taken care of."

"Seein' that changed how I looked at the world and what I wanted out of it—to be part of something bigger than outdoing the guy next to me," Gazlowe continued. "My whole crew will tell you we were proud of the job we did, and we were even prouder that we did it for the Horde." He tipped his glass to Noggenfogger. "Now I want to share that with you."

Noggenfogger frowned. "You want me to be proud of being a goblin?"

"I want *all* of us"—Gazlowe waved his hand to indicate all goblins in general—"to be proud of bein' goblins. I want us to be proud of what we can build, and I want the Horde to be proud to be associated with us! I want us to start lookin' to the future, to stop treatin' each other as enemies and understand that not everything is transactional, or a zero-sum game." He leaned back and put up his feet. "What we did back there at the site? Didja see how that mattered?"

"Yes. No. I don't know. How?"

Gazlowe gave a genial smile. "Because nothing changes the atmosphere—nothin' gains your people's respect—like a boss who wants to help and is willin' to learn and compromise. It'll move mountains."

Noggenfogger squinted at Gazlowe. "I just . . . still can't figure out your angle."

"No angle, buddy. If we don't start helpin' each other, we're

"I want us to be proud of what
we can build, and I want the Horde
to be proud to be associated with us!
I want us to start lookin' to the future,
to stop treatin' each other as enemies and
understand that not everything is
transactional, or a zero-sum game."

gonna tear each other apart until there's nothing left of us."

Noggenfogger didn't argue now; he looked as introspective as he was ever going to look. At that, he raised his glass. "To a new way."

"To a new way."

LITTLE SPARK

COURTNEY ALAMEDA

The star's light flickered, drawing a collective gasp from the soldiers on the training grounds outside Mereldar. The clash and clang of swords and shields wavered. Gazes turned starward. As the shadows stretched across the Dayspring Fields, fear stole prayers off lips. But just as suddenly, the star's light surged forth again. Faerin released a breath she didn't realize she'd been holding.

The star—Beledar—glowed with a light so bright, it matched the brilliance of the noonday sun. Or at least what Faerin could recall of the sun, having spent more than a decade hidden from its gaze. Unlike the sun, however, Beledar was an enormous crystal jutting down from the cavern's ceiling. All life in Hallowfall relied upon its light—a light that had been faltering of late, much to the horror of the Arathi.

Rumors ran wild in the barracks; soldiers speculated quietly that the people's faith in the Sacred Flame caused Beledar's instability. Faerin had even heard the *Order of Night* mentioned in low tones, but hadn't had the nerve to ask about what it was or how it affected Beledar.

Luckily, the star hadn't plunged all Hallowfall into darkness . . . *this time.*

"Carry on," General Vaelisia Steelstrike ordered from the parapet. The general seemed unperturbed by the star's flickering, her arms folded at the small of her back, shoulders straight, chin high. Only the deep furrow in her brow betrayed the depth of her concern.

Faerin stood on the grounds below, her javelin arm heavy from the day's exercises. Her cotton tunic clung to her skin, and her breastplate chafed. She rolled one shoulder, loosening her aching arm and back muscles. Unlike many of the reservists on the field, Faerin spent most of her time in training. After this session, she would change weapons and continue with another set of reserves.

As Faerin stretched her neck, she stole a glance at the person who stood beside Steelstrike with their arms crossed over their chest. Faerin knew them by reputation: the Great Kyron, leader of the enigmatic Lamplighters—an elite force of paladins who tested the boundaries of the darkness . . . and the limits of

Steelstrike's rules. When the Arathi crashed in Hallowfall, the Lamplighters had ventured into the darkness, beating back the nerubian threat and expanding the Arathi's foothold. But as Beledar's light began to flicker, the Lamplighters now served closer to home as well.

If there was anything Faerin wanted, it was to join their ranks.

Instead, she spent all her time training with the Arathi army under Steelstrike's watchful eye. Steelstrike had expectations for Faerin; a pity Faerin had little interest in meeting them.

"You heard the general." A stern voice drew Faerin's attention back to the training grounds. Meradyth Lacke, Faerin's training partner for the day, leveled her javelin at Faerin. "On guard, my lady."

My lady. Faerin bristled at those words. Meradyth, a mere reservist who spent her time holed up reading in the Priory of the Sacred Flame, rather than on the front lines. Meradyth, one of the few who insisted on calling Faerin by her "title." The formality didn't suit her, and not just because of her age. Faerin was the youngest soldier on the field by at least a decade, perhaps more. Her comrades-in-arms were not keen on being led by a youth, no matter which bloodline she could claim. After all, old titles couldn't stave off the darkness—only the Sacred Flame could do that.

"I've told you not to call me that," Faerin shot back.

"But it *is* your title—"

"A technicality," Faerin replied. "Nothing more."

Meradyth merely shrugged. "I will not break with tradition, I'm afraid."

"Pity." Faerin grinned, brandishing her javelin. "Think you can keep up this time? In our last bout, I struck the javelin from your hands and nearly knocked you prone."

"That was little more than luck." Meradyth sniffed. "You made use of an unsanctioned technique to disarm me. We've orders to practice a set of *approved* maneuvers, Lady Faerin."

Faerin ground her teeth. The creatures in the darkness had no such formalities or rules of combat. "You let me in too close, and I got a knee under your leg." Faerin twirled her javelin. Its sharp tip whistled as it cleaved the air. "Survival in battle requires resourcefulness—especially against the nerubians."

"A weak justification," Meradyth replied, narrowing her eyes. "I suppose it's understandable—it must be difficult to perform our most sacred martial techniques one-handed."

Faerin scoffed. True, she had lost more than half her arm in the crash that brought the Arathi to Hallowfall, along with the sight in her left eye. True, there were techniques with sword and shield Faerin would never master, for she could not wield both at once. True, the lack of a left arm forced her to approach the battlefield differently than her comrades. But it was wrong to imply that Faerin used a little improvisation on the battlefield simply because she couldn't perform certain martial techniques; and even if that *were* true, there was no dishonor in it.

She was no less a warrior for her scars. It seemed Meradyth needed a reminder.

Without another word, Faerin swept the point of her javelin down, taking her sparring partner by surprise. She took a cross step to the left to avoid a counterthrust, then slammed the shaft of her weapon into Meradyth's, knocking the point of the older woman's javelin skyward. Meradyth took a step back in surprise, leaving herself exposed. In another step, Faerin leveled her javelin at Meradyth's throat. Meradyth swallowed hard, her eyes widening.

"You question my methods," Faerin said, "and yet you fail to keep pace."

"Again, you dispense with our martial tradition in the name of your stubborn pride," Meradyth replied, her words stinging. "Such obstinance would be punished harshly at home."

"But we're not at home, are we?" Faerin moved her javelin tip from Meradyth's throat. She slammed the butt of the weapon into the ground with a thud and stood taller.

From the parapet, Steelstrike gave Faerin a nod. General Steelstrike was both the leader of the Arathi forces and Faerin's reluctant guardian. It was she who had found Faerin in the hull

"Again, you dispense with our martial tradition in the name of your stubborn pride," Meradyth replied, her words stinging. "Such obstinance would be punished harshly at home."

"But we're not at home, are we?" Faerin moved her javelin tip from Meradyth's throat. She slammed the butt of the weapon into the ground with a thud and stood taller.

of her airship after the crash that brought them here so long ago. Despite her gruff demeanor, the general had held Faerin's hand while the healers cut her free from the wreckage and cauterized her wounds.

The general had been keeping a close eye on Faerin as she'd grown, and not just because many soldiers and reservists had qualms about Faerin's . . . *iconoclast* style. Steelstrike had taken a liking to her over the years—having already offered her an opportunity to become an officer . . . provided she could rein in her more *reckless* tendencies. Faerin had demurred, not ready to relinquish her freedoms.

Faerin noticed the Great Kyron was now accompanied by a second Lamplighter, one who went by the name Andari. *What are they doing here?* Faerin wondered, slamming the point of her javelin into the ground and shucking off her training gauntlet. *Shouldn't they have better things to do?* Still, a little thrill raced through Faerin. Now, the leader of the Lamplighters and one of its most promising lieutenants had seen her fight. Steelstrike had forbidden Faerin from joining the Lamplighters, saying that her considerable talents would be wasted on Lamplighter work, but maybe the Great Kyron would overrule her.

"Our traditions keep us strong. Though we are far from our ancestral land, we are still part of the great Arathi empire," Meradyth said, gesturing to her imperial lynx, Stoutheart, who waited on the sidelines. He was one of the giant cats the Arathi soldiers bonded with and rode into battle. "Perhaps *this* is why our imperial lynxes eschew your company. Even they can sense your faithlessness."

"Strange that you invoke faith, given your inability to wield the Sacred Flame," Faerin said, knowing full well her words would strike a nerve. Though Meradyth spent most of her days at the Priory, she possessed no facility with the Sacred Flame. She could neither channel its Light to smite an enemy nor wrap its warmth around a wound. For all Meradyth's faith, that power refused to answer her call.

That brilliant power, however, flowed through Faerin with ease.

"How dare you." Embarrassment splotched across Meradyth's pallid face. In the span of a moment, she lunged forward and thrust her javelin at Faerin—a wild attack.

Faerin sidestepped and struck Meradyth in the sternum with the blunt end of her javelin. Meradyth staggered back a step, pressing one hand into her chest. Her lynx hissed, bearing its long teeth, as if the creature felt Faerin's jab too. Meradyth glared, huffing for breath.

"You," she told Faerin, "fail to see the precariousness of our situation—"

"On the contrary, I see our situation quite clearly." Faerin

*Avoid the darkness. Stay in
the light,* Steelstrike often said.
Those were two of the many rules
the general and her staff had instilled
in the Arathi people . . . and the one Faerin
struggled to follow. The Lamplighters strode
fearlessly into the unknown, bearing the
light for their brethren and fighting the
terrors that thrived in the dark.
Why should she not go and
do likewise?

narrowed her sighted eye at Meradyth and her agitated lynx. "I am the first to come of age beneath Beledar's light. And though I remember and honor the empire's edicts, my faith is vested in the Sacred Flame itself."

Just as those words left her lips, the star shifted into shadow. Darkness spilled across the training grounds.

Cries of fear echoed against the city's stone walls.

Faerin's heart seized. The star throbbed with violet light, shrouding Hallowfall in horrifying midnight. Meradyth's blonde hair glowed a silvery lavender in the crystal's twisted glow, as did the battered plate armor of the soldiers who surrounded her.

Up on the city's parapets, Kyron shouted: "Light the lamps! Light the lamps!"

"Everyone inside, and quickly!" General Steelstrike cried.

Avoid the darkness. Stay in the light, Steelstrike often said. Those were two of the many rules the general and her staff had instilled in the Arathi people . . . and the one Faerin struggled to follow. The Lamplighters strode fearlessly into the unknown, bearing the light for their brethren and fighting the terrors that thrived in the dark. Why should she not go and do likewise?

Without another word, Meradyth mounted her lynx and trotted off to join the retreating throng.

In the distance, pairs of Lamplighters lit the dawntowers.

LITTLE SPARK

The braziers sparked to life, their growing light pushing back against the darkness. A great hum filled the air as the Arathi airships took to the sky, their fore and aft lights twinkling like long-gone stars in the firmament. Should the bloodthirsty nerubians choose to strike in the darkness, the artillery aboard the airships would defend both Mereldar and the Arathi's outlying settlements.

Faerin's heart beat a little harder. *Avoid the darkness.* This edict came before all others, and the general expected everyone to obey it without question. Still, Faerin hesitated—the sudden onslaught of darkness struck fear into even her courageous heart.

Reservists pushed past her, heading for the gates. Since the Arathi's arrival, the nerubians had laid constant siege to Mereldar and the city's surrounding settlements, waging a never-ending war of attrition against her people. Still, they had yet to quench the Arathi flame. The Arathi had held on . . . but *barely.* Every battle counted, no matter how large or small.

"Move! Get inside!" a soldier called out to the others. "Now!"

Stay in the light. But what if she wished to carry the Light into the darkness?

"Hey!" Ryton Blackholme playfully knocked a shoulder into hers. She grunted, but grinned. Though the paladin was deep in his thirties, Ryton still had a youthful air, a cheekiness that often made Faerin feel more like his eye-rolling older sister. "You heard the general. Inside we go."

"You're altogether too pleased to abandon training for an afternoon," Faerin said, sheathing her javelin and following him.

"What can I say?" He spread his arms wide as he took a few steps ahead. "I have a mountain of orders to see to, but I wouldn't say no to an afternoon drinking with my comrades either. We're all stuck down here for Flame knows how long. Might as well enjoy ourselves."

Over the last decade, the paladin had become as good at forging swords as he was at swinging them, which was to say very, *very* good. While the Arathi of Hallowfall had many smiths, Ryton was one of their best . . . and he was the closest thing to a friend Faerin had ever known. His very presence soothed her.

As she and Ryton joined the crowd heading for the gates, tension strung every conversation taut. While the Arathi had grown accustomed to Beledar shifting, it made them no less anxious. The fear was palpable. Everywhere. Whispers of the shift heralding Renilash, the final battle between light and dark . . . the end of the world . . .

"I must admit," Faerin said to Ryton, trying to shrug off the fear, "I don't relish the idea of a long lockdown with the general."

Ryton chuckled. "Aye, she'll have her own ideas on how

we should keep busy. I suppose she'll make us shelter at the barracks, however long the darkness might stay."

"Or the Priory." Faerin made a face, watching Meradyth not far ahead in the line. "That might be worse—"

Panicked shouts interrupted them, echoing off the nearby cliffs. The closest airship signaled a warning to those below. Someone on board must have spotted an attack.

Nerubians. Here? Most nerubian attacks occurred at the Aegis Wall, far from Mereldar's front gates. Faerin braced herself with her javelin. Her heart started to pound, flooding her body with adrenaline and sharpening every sense.

Ryton pushed her forward, unsheathing the sword at his waist. "Go, Faerin! *Run.*" He gestured to the city gates. "There's no need for you to risk your life out here."

"And leave you to have all the fun?" Faerin said, glad her voice didn't crack with fear.

"You're barely of age, no more than a little spark," he said.

"I've already seen my fair share of battles," Faerin countered, switching the grip on her javelin and tensing for a fight. "You forget I was raised by the army."

Ryton rolled his eyes, but the grin never left his lips. "Come on, then, *little spark*. Let's see how much trouble we can raise!"

They raced to the nearest cliff's edge, where nerubians swarmed up and clashed with Arathi soldiers. Steel flashed in

Beledar's unsettling violet light. Screams rent the air. Faerin gripped her javelin, her palm already slick with sweat.

Before she could press the attack, a nerubian warrior leaped at her. The beast towered some twelve feet tall. Each of its six legs ended in sharp, wedge-shaped points, and massive pincers clicked from its mandible. The warrior's bony carapaces were hard as steel, nigh unto impenetrable.

"Faerin, on your left!" Ryton shouted.

Heeding her comrade's warning, Faerin spun. A second warrior rushed at them, its gemlike eyes flashing wickedly. Perhaps it meant to take advantage of what appeared to be an opening on her left side. If the creature had been canny, it would have realized Faerin's lack of a shield arm hardly hampered her on the battlefield.

With a shriek, the warrior leaped at Faerin, covering five yards in a single bound. It swiped both forearms, trying to trap her in a pincer move.

She turned her javelin perpendicular to her chest to catch the creature's claws on its shaft. As the warrior bore down, she twisted her wrist to turn the weapon's point toward the ground, using the nerubian's own strength and momentum to flip the tip of the javelin toward its torso. The weapon moved with such force, it cracked the nerubian's carapace.

In the next heartbeat, she placed the butt of her javelin

against her right hip, twisted her body, and drove it between the warrior's armored plates. The heavy blade crunched through the warrior's exoskeleton, slicing into its innards with a sickening *squelch*.

The creature shrieked in pain—a high-frequency sound that would make even the most seasoned fighter wince, but Faerin was born for battle. Moments like these made her feel alive—the realization of her training, proof of her martial mastery.

Death snuffed out the cruel light in the creature's eyes.

"That's one for me," she shouted at Ryton, jerking her weapon free.

The blacksmith acknowledged her victory with a grunt, pushing the first warrior back toward the cliff—the nerubian had already lost an arm to Ryton's blade. Its dismembered limb writhed on the ground, its clawed fist flexing. Faerin kicked it away.

As the warrior moved to strike, a massive shadow leaped from behind. It slammed into the warrior's torso—shrieking, biting, and clawing—forcing the nerubian to the ground. Ryton's massive lynx, Blazeclaw, mauled the nerubian's head with her sickled claws, giving Ryton an opening to drive his blade into the monster's chest.

"Good girl!" Ryton shouted.

Along the parapet, more braziers flared to life, creating a

"Come! They've called the retreat," Ryton called out, climbing into Blazeclaw's saddle. Nerubian blood stained the lynx's muzzle and giant paws. Ryton extended a hand to Faerin as the big cat sidled close. "We can't stay."

Faerin sheathed her javelin and clapped her hand in his. Before he could pull her astride, a scream caught Faerin's attention.

wall of light around the city's outer defenses. The line of nerubian warriors skittered into the shadows, seeking sanctuary. An airship soared above the signal fires, sending a volley of artillery into the nerubians' backs. The fire burned so hot, the nerubians' carapaces bubbled and cracked. The heat bristled against Faerin's skin, and the shadows of the dying danced along the city's walls.

Over the hissing, Faerin could barely hear the horns sounding the retreat.

"Come! They've called the retreat," Ryton called out, climbing into Blazeclaw's saddle. Nerubian blood stained the lynx's muzzle and giant paws. Ryton extended a hand to Faerin as the big cat sidled close. "We can't stay."

Faerin sheathed her javelin and clapped her hand in his. Before he could pull her astride, a scream caught Faerin's attention.

Near the city's walls, larger nerubians lassoed Arathi soldiers with long, sticky strands of spider's silk. One by one, the soldiers were yanked into the darkness, shrieking for aid. Among the trapped was Meradyth, now separated from her lynx, her left leg wrapped in gauzy white silk. She clung to a training dummy to avoid being hauled into the shadows. Another of her comrades, Andryck, sheltered in a nearby outbuilding, straining to tear the webs from his armor.

Faerin stepped back, slipping her hand out of Ryton's.

"Leave them," he shouted. "They are already lost!"

"I cannot," Faerin said. "Not while they still draw breath!" Steelstrike's soldiers followed her rules . . . but Faerin was about to break the most important one.

Avoid the darkness.

Faerin charged headlong toward her comrades. Into the shadows. Collecting the Sacred Flame in her hand, she jettisoned it toward the nerubians in a whirl of divine energy. Three hammers of Light spiraled outward from Faerin, hiting all five at once. The Light sliced through the webs, freeing the trapped soldiers. The nerubians turned toward her, hissing.

"Run!" Faerin shouted at the soldiers, yanking her javelin from its sheath. "Go!"

Many of the freed gave her a nod, shouting their thanks, but Meradyth didn't move. She clung to the training dummy, her face buried in its battered chest.

"Go, Meradyth!" Faerin shouted.

If Meradyth heard her, she made no sign.

Dammit! As the beasts swarmed close, Faerin stabbed her javelin into the earth. With a shout, she sent a bolt of Sacred Flame through the end, consecrating the soil underfoot. Lines of golden Light shattered the ground, chasing the swarm back.

Wrenching her javelin free, Faerin took stock of her enemy: There were five nerubians within range, inching toward the edge of her consecration. If she stunned them, she might have enough time to get Meradyth to safety . . . assuming one of the creatures didn't try to snatch and drag them both into the darkness. Their survival now balanced on a knife's edge.

With a prayer on her lips, Faerin spun, sending a blinding hammer of Holy Light whirling through the air around her. Each time it connected with the nerubians' vile hides, it set off a flash of brilliance and pealed like a bell.

Faerin did not wait. Sheathing her javelin, she grabbed Meradyth by the hand and *ran.* She pushed the older soldier ahead, shouting at her to flee.

As they sprinted for the city's gates, Ryton and Blazeclaw appeared from the darkness. Ryton leaped down before they reached him, grabbed Meradyth as if she were no more than a child, and threw her onto the lynx's saddle.

"You next, little spark," Ryton said, hauling Faerin into the saddle behind Meradyth. Ryton tried to leap up behind them, but the shadows moved quicker. Two nerubians materialized through the smoke. One charged at Blazeclaw, while the other dove at Ryton with an earsplitting shriek.

Faerin stretched forth her hand, calling the Sacred Flame to protect them. It exploded from her fingertips in a glittering hammer, slamming into one of the nerubians. Faerin hadn't enough time to stop the second warrior, however. It pounced upon Ryton, knocking the paladin prostrate. His sword clattered out of reach. The nerubian snatched him by the breastplate and dragged him backward, straight into the shadows.

"Go!" Ryton cried as the darkness swallowed him.

Meradyth snapped Blazeclaw's reins, and the lynx surged forward.

Faerin screamed, her voice raw with rage. Before she could call down the Sacred Flame to shield her friend, the lynx leaped toward Mereldar, the shadows obscuring everything behind them.

"No," Faerin whispered. *"No."*

As they rode through the main gate, Blazeclaw slid to a stop, shook both women off her back, and turned again to the battlefield. Before she could go after her master, the heavy portcullis came crashing down, sealing everyone inside. The lynx roared and hooked her claws into the gate, but not even Blazeclaw could rend Arathi iron in twain.

Faerin pushed to her feet, her heart on fire. "You left him," she said to Meradyth. "You left him out there to *die.*"

"As you should have left *me,*" Meradyth said, dusting her hands together. "There are consequences for breaking the rules, Lady Faerin—perhaps *this* will finally help you understand that our rules exist for a reason, and that *none* of us are above them. Not even you."

"Go!" Ryton cried
as the darkness swallowed him.
Meradyth snapped Blazeclaw's reins,
and the lynx surged forward.

Faerin screamed, her voice raw with
rage. Before she could call down the
Sacred Flame to shield her friend, the
lynx leaped toward Mereldar, the
shadows obscuring everything
behind them.

"Is that how you thank me?" Faerin said through gritted teeth. "You were too terrified to move out there, and had I not intervened—"

"Let me finish that statement for you," Meradyth said, her tone grim. "Had you not intervened, Mereldar's best blacksmith would *still be alive.*"

Her words hit Faerin harder than a physical blow, piercing places that steel could never hope to reach. Faerin took a step back, fighting a great trembling sob.

"Think on that, next time you decide to play hero," Meradyth said bitterly.

Blazeclaw sat before the gate and let out a low, mournful cry.

"Private Faerin," someone shouted.

Faerin cursed under her breath. She knew that grizzled voice too well—General Steelstrike.

Faerin lifted her chin and squared her shoulders.

"General," Faerin said by way of greeting, blinking hard to keep the tears from streaking down her cheeks. Meradyth saluted Steelstrike and stepped back, leaving Faerin alone to face her. Faerin was keenly aware of the soldiers who watched them from the walls too—every eye focused on her.

"What were you *thinking?*" Steelstrike said, her brow furrowing. "You should have fallen back when the retreat was sounded! We lost one of our own to your foolishness!" She glanced at Meradyth for a second. "The careless perish, Private Faerin. You know this."

"With all due respect, what would you have me do?" she said, gesturing to Meradyth. "She clearly needed help—"

"I had accepted my fate and was prepared to give my life, as always," Meradyth snapped.

"Nonsense," Faerin spat. "You cowered like a *child* before the enemy!"

"Silence!" Steelstrike narrowed her eyes as she stepped forward. "I will not have such impertinence and division in my ranks! If we are to survive, we must work together—"

"And that's *precisely* why I went back for Meradyth and the others," Faerin said.

"Enough," Steelstrike snapped, pinning Faerin with a gaze. "One more insolent word out of you, and I'll have you tried for sedition. Is that clear?"

Faerin held that cold glare, flaring her nostrils. Steelstrike's reprimand stung, but Faerin knew better than to be openly defiant of the general in public. The Arathi could ill afford more contention and dissent in their ranks, especially as it pertained to her.

"Yes, ma'am. I am sorry, ma'am." Her words were practiced, formal; but Steelstrike knew her well enough to sense the impertinence in them.

The general turned her attention to Meradyth next. "Meradyth Lacke," Steelstrike said, folding her hands behind her back. "Since you seem to have a better grasp on the rules than our dear Private Faerin, you are to accompany her on all her duties going forward—"

"What?" Faerin and Meradyth cried out, almost in unison.

Steelstrike gave Faerin a sharp look, warning her not to test her patience a third time. "She will temper your heroics, Private Faerin," the general said. "A brittle blade shatters at first strike, even when wielded with confidence."

Faerin stepped forward, gesturing with her hand. "But—"

"Very good." With that, Steelstrike turned away, ordering everyone inside.

Faerin shot a glance at Meradyth, who scowled. She had traded her friend, the best blacksmith in Mereldar, for an ungrateful coward whom even the Sacred Flame had forsaken.

"I do not like this any more than you do, Lady Faerin."

Faerin clenched her jaw. "Next time you're in danger, save yourself."

Hours passed. As soon as Beledar's light flared bright again, Faerin snuck from the barracks. Though Steelstrike had ordered the troops to shelter in their quarters until the light proved stable, Faerin refused to abandon Ryton to darkness and death.

Faerin tightened a strap on her armor, waiting in the shadows of Mereldar's walls. Watchful. Nervous. Both Eoghan Knatley and Andryck Carltyn had agreed to help her search for Ryton, as the two men were the blacksmith's oldest friends. The trio had planned to meet a few hours after dinner, during a change in the guard and after the reservists had gone to bed. Fewer eyes meant fewer chances of being spotted, even in the light.

Some of the tension in her muscles eased as she caught a glimpse of Eoghan and Andryck, creeping close to the walls. They were accompanied by four imperial lynxes, one of which walked with its head hung, ears flat, tail drooping. *Blazeclaw.*

"Did the stablehands give you any trouble with Blazeclaw?" Faerin asked as they approached. She reached out and scratched the sensitive little spot behind the cat's ears, sensing a deep sadness within the creature.

Eoghan smiled a bit sadly. "The stablemaster owes me a favor, but even if he didn't . . . he was fond of Ryton too."

The blacksmith had many friends in Mereldar. Faerin looked to Andryck. "And the airship?"

"I managed to talk one of the captains into modifying the clearance orders for a patrol tonight," he replied, holding up a

"We will find Ryton, if he lives," Faerin said, ruffling the thick, soft fur around Blazeclaw's neck. "Now quickly, before—"

"Before *what*?" someone snapped. Meradyth emerged from a darkened alleyway with her lynx, her fury written in the deep lines on her forehead.

parchment bound in leather. "They won't give us any trouble."

"We will find Ryton, if he lives," Faerin said, ruffling the thick, soft fur around Blazeclaw's neck. "Now quickly, before—"

"Before *what*?" someone snapped. Meradyth emerged from a darkened alleyway with her lynx, her fury written in the deep lines on her forehead.

Faerin curled her lip, frustration rising. Eoghan cursed under his breath.

"I knew something was amiss when you weren't abed, Lady Faerin," Meradyth said, looking from Faerin to Andryck. "What are you doing, dressed for battle and traveling with Ryton's lynx? . . . Don't tell me you mean to go after the man."

"Fine, then I won't," Faerin said.

"Ryton is *lost*." Though Meradyth tried to sound firm, a hitch of fear rose in her voice. Perhaps it was the way her tone pitched higher at the end of her sentence, or the flutter of the big veins in her throat. Faerin gritted her teeth in annoyance, keeping her expression blank.

"Hope yet remains." Andryck tucked their patrol orders away. "Scouts have reported activity in the tunnels near Beledar's Bounty, including Arathi tracks. Ryton might have a chance if—"

"He *doesn't* have a chance," Meradyth said. "None of us do, not outside the city's walls! That's why we must stay—"

"Then stay!" Faerin said through her teeth. "Cower behind Mereldar's walls if you must! No one asked for your help, Meradyth."

"We're not reservists," Andryck added, but his tone was gentler. "We are well accustomed to fighting the nerubians. Should it come to violence, the three of us could easily handle a small swarm."

"This is madness." Meradyth turned on her heel. "I'm going to Steelstrike."

"Excellent," Faerin replied, placing her gauntleted fist on one hip. "See how well she takes the news that you've let me slip through your fingers, failing in your new duties in mere *hours*."

Meradyth halted but did not turn. Her lynx let out a low growl. "This isn't a duty," she said, fisting her hands at her sides.

"Andryck has orders in hand for a patrol," Faerin continued, softer now.

Meradyth shuddered, sinking her fingers into her lynx's thick fur. The big cat, Stoutheart, trilled, bumping its forehead against her shoulder.

After what felt like an age, Meradyth spoke: "Since your minds are made up, I will go with you."

Faerin gritted her teeth but said nothing. She had hoped Meradyth would lose her courage, but the woman *was* an Arathi, after all.

"However," Meradyth continued, "if I concede this to you, Lady Faerin, you must promise me that you will turn back if Ryton's trail leads beyond Arathi holdings."

"I can promise you that much," Faerin replied.

"Very well," Meradyth said, patting her lynx. "Let us be off, then."

"Look there!" Faerin stood in the airship's bow, pointing to the village of Beledar's Bounty. Fires winked like lynxes' eyes. Long columns of smoke rose into the air, and the land lay battered beneath them. The smoke made Faerin's eyes water, and the air smelled like char. "Andryck, can you bring us closer?"

"Aye." Andryck pulled a lever. The airship began to descend.

Meradyth joined Faerin in the bow, frowning at the scene below. The woman braced herself against the airship's railing. "I mislike this. It feels like a trap."

"The nerubians wouldn't tarry, especially in Beledar's light," Faerin replied. "No, this was banditry at best, vengeance at worst."

As the airship neared the ground, the lynxes rose and stretched. The cats were well equipped for riding airships.

Most soldiers had bonded with one, save for Faerin, who had yet to receive the honor of such a companion. Instead, she rode hirelings.

As the airship touched down, Faerin's current beast of burden looked at her with annoyance. *Only a cat could look so cross*, she thought.

Faerin and her companions mounted up and disembarked. To their dismay, they found naught but destruction—trampled fields, shattered outbuildings, decimated herds. Nerubian tracks crisscrossed the paths. Inside a shattered cottage, Faerin found two corpses, bled out and barely more than bones. She whispered prayers over their bodies, hoping they would find rest in the Sacred Flame.

As she stepped outside, she glanced down at her glove. Blood—thick and dark as garnet—now stained her fingers. Fragments of spider's silk clung to the toes of her boots. Two dead . . . but that was not nearly enough to account for the bulk of the settlement.

While such attacks might be rare closer to Mereldar, Beledar's Bounty was often the target of nerubian raids. The place was little more than an outpost to house those who worked the Arathi's prized farmlands. The settlement would need to be rebuilt and quickly fortified, or their holdings here would be lost.

As she stepped outside,
she glanced down at her glove.
Blood—thick and dark as garnet
—now stained her fingers. Fragments
of spider's silk clung to the toes of her
boots. Two dead . . . but that was not
nearly enough to account for the
bulk of the settlement.

"Lady Faerin, we must tell the general of this attack," Meradyth cut in. "We should return to Mereldar at once."

"If we do not act, lives will be lost," Faerin said, nodding to the tracks that led from the settlement. "We press forward."

"And if we do not inform the officers of the village's predicament, our fields lie open to attack," Meradyth countered.

Unfortunately, the woman had a point. Faerin sighed. "Fine. Eoghan, Andryck, light the village's signal flares and rendezvous with us at your earliest opportunity. Meradyth and I will track the nerubians—they must have retreated to a cavern nearby."

Meradyth looked two shades too pale, but she did not argue. They bade Eoghan and Andryck farewell. Faerin gave Blazeclaw a command to track her master, then followed the great cat on foot, leading her hireling lynx by the reins. Unlike Meradyth's great cat, Stoutheart, a hireling lynx would not follow Faerin out of loyalty, nor would it fight at her side. Only a bonded cat would do that.

The nerubians' tracks descended into a nearby canyon, running down a thin ledge along the cliff's face. The trail looked treacherous. A misstep would send one plummeting into the deep shadows below, where nerubians and kobyss likely lurked.

The deeper Faerin and Meradyth ventured, the weaker

LITTLE SPARK

Beledar's light grew. "We should turn back," Meradyth said. "If Beledar were to shift while we cling to this cliffside . . ."

"Beledar's light will hold," Faerin replied, using her hand to brace herself against the rocky wall.

"Hmph," Meradyth said. "We should not gamble with the light, Lady Faerin. The star shifts suddenly, unexpectedly. I do not wish to be caught in darkness."

"By the Flame," Faerin muttered, reining in her lynx and halting on the trail. "Why are you so desperate to return to Mereldar? Are you truly so afraid of breaking even a single rule?"

Meradyth scoffed, but said nothing more.

The trail widened, taking a sharp turn into a hollow section of the cliff. The mouth of a massive cavern yawned wide, draped in shadows and spider's silk. Inside, the darkness thickened, and scraggly trees withered away to spindles. Even Beledar's rays struggled to penetrate a gloom so deep.

The light touched upon the skeletal remains of an Arathi airship, pillaged for parts and left to rot. Faerin wondered if it had been one of the expedition's original ships—it had none of the innovations that made modern aircraft fit for underground flight. She could barely make out the words *The Valiant Ghost* on its stern.

A shudder trailed down her spine. At eight years old, Faerin

In those moments,
she prayed for salvation,
clinging to a fragile spark of hope.
That hope had materialized in the
form of General Steelstrike, from a face
not taut with fear but hardened with
resolve. With courage. The general's
resolve had forged Faerin's faith,
kindling the Sacred Flame inside
her from a little spark into
a full blaze.

had stowed away in the hull of General Steelstrike's airship, dreaming of adventure. Instead, she found only darkness, danger, and despair. The sight of the wreckage dredged up memories of the Arathi's disastrous arrival in Hallowfall, memories she would rather forget.

Faerin's stomach lurched as she remembered a bright flash of light. As the airship plummeted from the skies, a despicable feeling of weightlessness stole the very air from her lungs. She had fallen for seconds; she had fallen forever, only to feel the airship shatter as if her own bones broke upon Hallowfall's fjords.

Then came the darkness—complete, absolute—followed by hours of agonizing pain as Faerin lay trapped under the ship's rubble. In those moments, she prayed for salvation, clinging to a fragile spark of hope. That hope had materialized in the form of General Steelstrike, from a face not taut with fear but hardened with resolve. With *courage.* The general's resolve had forged Faerin's faith, kindling the Sacred Flame inside her from a little spark into a full blaze. And while she might balk at the general's litany of rules, she had to admit that she found the woman's ironclad courage and tenacity inspiring.

The Sacred Flame had guided Steelstrike to Faerin in her darkest hour, and it would ever light her path. So Faerin would find Ryton and the survivors of Beledar's Bounty . . . no matter the odds.

Footsteps tugged Faerin from her memories. She wiped the back of her hand under her nose.

"Are you all right?" Meradyth joined her at the precipice of the cavern.

Faerin cleared her throat. "I'm fine."

"I see no sign of survivors. Our duty here is done." Meradyth scanned the cavern. Her eyes widened as she observed the ship. "Wait, is that . . . *The Valiant Ghost*?" she asked with a gasp.

"It was," Faerin replied.

"Impossible." Meradyth blinked rapidly, chin quivering. She took another step toward the shadows. "Surely the ship had been found . . . surely her dead have been laid to rest? But no one said a word to me, even at the Priory . . ." With a soft sob, Meradyth stepped inside the cavern. The shadows within slipped over the toes of her boots. Ancient webs crumbled under her steps while the last of Beledar's light still gleamed off the back of her breastplate.

"How many of our ships were lost to the shadows?" Meradyth whispered, taking another step inside. "We came here in faith, you and I, but only one of us still walks in the warmth of the Sacred Flame."

Somehow, Faerin knew Meradyth wasn't talking to her—not anymore.

With another step, the silk under Meradyth's feet began to

shear away, revealing a dark crack in the cavern's natural floor.

Meradyth cried out and scrambled back, but the spider's silk clung to her boots. In her panic, she thrashed, snapping the delicate threads. The webs bowed beneath her weight.

Before Faerin could lunge forward, the webs tore. Meradyth tumbled into a hidden crevasse in the floor, screaming.

"Meradyth!" Faerin cried. With a yowl, Stoutheart leaped to the ledge. He extended one of his great forepaws into the darkness below, only to release a throaty growl when he could not reach his rider. Twitching his bobbed tail, the big cat began pacing back and forth along the ledge. He looked to Faerin, then to the crevasse, then to Faerin again as if to say, *Well, don't just stand there! Do something!*

Faerin fell on her knees at the edge, sending pebbles skittering. The darkness had swallowed Meradyth whole. Dust whorled in her wake, and a shroud of ancient, moldering webs now flitted like tattered flags over the opening. *A trap*, Faerin thought, rubbing a bit of spider's silk between her fingers. It crumbled to the touch, perhaps forgotten by even the nerubians themselves.

A sob reached up from the shadows.

"Meradyth?" Faerin called, keeping her voice low. "Are you hurt?"

"Just bruised, I-I think," Meradyth said, half-choked and

hiccupping. Words tumbled out of her so fast that Faerin could barely make sense of them: "It's dark, it's so dark," she sobbed to herself. "I can't breathe in this. Flame help me, please, please . . ."

"Meradyth," Faerin called to her. "Can you feel a foothold, something to grab on to, anything?"

"I can't," Meradyth cried, panicked. "I-I'm sorry, I can't, it's so dark—"

"You *must*," Faerin shouted. "Reach up."

"The darkness . . . I-I can hardly breathe, I—"

The memory of being trapped in the dark rolled through Faerin, accompanied by a wave of nausea. She closed her eyes and turned her head, waiting for the feeling to pass. She, too, had begged for freedom, for relief . . . but it had been days before Steelstrike heard her cries.

"Please," Meradyth said, her voice breathy, panicked. "I know that I've been nothing but a thorn in your side, but you can't leave me down here. I-I . . . I have a terrible fear of the dark."

As do we all. Was *this* why Meradyth clung to the rules so tightly? Why she hadn't been able to flee during the attack?

With a sigh, Faerin pushed back to her feet. Stoutheart turned his big head to her, flattening his ears along his skull. The cat growled as she turned away.

"No, wait," Meradyth said. "Where are you going?"

Faerin didn't answer.

"Lady Faerin? Faerin, *please*! Don't leave me down here . . ."

Faerin stalked a few steps into the cavern's shadows, grabbing a long, dusty length of rope. As Meradyth begged and pleaded for deliverance, Faerin looped the rope around a nearby stalagmite, made a deft knot around its trunk, and picked up the remaining coils.

Faerin returned to the ledge. Meradyth's sobs echoed through the whole of the cavern now, throaty and jagged.

"The next time you tell me to follow a rule instead of saving a life, I want you to remember this moment," Faerin said, then dropped the rope into the darkness. It hit the bottom with a solid *thwack*.

In mere moments, Meradyth scrambled to safety with nary a *thank-you*. The woman stumbled from the crevasse and collapsed in a small, dim puddle of Beledar's light, chest heaving, arms shaking. Stoutheart lay beside her, curling his body around her back. Protective.

Faerin stepped from the cave, turning her face to the skies and soaking in the star's light. Even in a place like this, Beledar's warmth flooded her mind and eased the horrors of her past. She closed her eyes, drew in a deep breath, and said a silent prayer of gratitude.

As Meradyth's sobs stilled, Faerin opened her eyes. "Where were you?" she asked.

"What?" Meradyth replied with a sniffle.

"Your fear of the dark—it must have come from the crash. Were you aboard *The Valiant Ghost* or another airship entirely?"

Meradyth turned toward Faerin but did not lift her gaze. Instead, her blank-eyed stare seemed to focus on something a thousand leagues away. Blood bubbled from one of her temples. Webs clung to her armor and hair. After a moment, she said, "My sister and I were separated for the expedition—she was aboard *The Valiant Ghost*. Like you, she was naturally proficient with the Light. Brave, kind, true. She did not deserve to die here in darkness."

"No one deserves such a fate." Faerin turned her gaze back to the wreckage, remembering her own dark hours. What Meradyth couldn't understand was that Faerin didn't break every rule in General Steelstrike's vast repertoire out of a need to play the hero, or some foolhardy desire to prove herself. No, Faerin broke the general's rules because they had once been broken for *her*. She, too, had faced the unblinking shadows, trapped and powerless. She knew what it meant to keep hope alive even in the depths of despair, to be pulled from the darkness, and to become the hand that could save others from its grasp.

No, Faerin broke
the general's rules because
they had once been broken for her.
She, too, had faced the unblinking
shadows, trapped and powerless. She
knew what it meant to keep hope alive
even in the depths of despair, to be
pulled from the darkness, and to
become the hand that could save
others from its grasp.

But beneath it all, she knew her fear of the dark could never be greater than her faith in the Sacred Flame.

Little spark, Ryton whispered in her mind, but his memory gave her no answers.

With a sigh, Faerin stood. She no longer saw Meradyth as a self-righteous coward, but as a survivor still very much trapped in the wreckage, so many years on. Perhaps the crash that ignited the Flame within Faerin had snuffed out the same spark within Meradyth.

"Lady Faerin?"

Faerin halted and glanced over her shoulder.

"I should thank you," Meradyth said, bowing her head. "And I should apologize, too, for not being grateful back at the gate. Though I will never condone what you did . . . I am thankful I still draw breath."

"You can thank me by never calling me *lady* again," Faerin replied.

"I cannot make such a promise." Meradyth shook her head. "The blood of the empire still runs in your veins."

Faerin snorted, but before she could reply, Ryton's lynx, Blazeclaw, made a low growl in the back of her throat. The big cat stalked toward the cavern, ears flat, bobbed tail twitching.

"Blazeclaw?" Faerin asked, eyeing the cavern's shadows. "What's the matter?"

LITTLE SPARK

The lynx stepped forward, curling its lips over its fangs.

A thin wail rose from the cavern's shadows. With a snarl, Blazeclaw leaped forward. Faerin scrambled into her lynx's saddle, shouting after the big cat. As Ryton's mount disappeared into the shadows, Faerin leaped after her.

"Lady Faerin," Meradyth shrieked. "Wait!"

Faerin reined her lynx in, glancing over her shoulder at Meradyth. "I will go without you if I must," Faerin said, igniting the lantern that hung from her lynx's saddle. "But you can be so much more than this, Meradyth. You can be so much braver, so much stronger. You still walk in the Light of the Sacred Flame, even when you are surrounded by shadows."

There was a beat, a pause that made Faerin think Meradyth would deny her yet.

With a glance back at Beledar's light, Meradyth said, "It's wrong to break the general's rules, but you are right. We cannot abandon our allies to darkness and despair. I will ride with you, Lady Faerin."

Faerin reached down and unhooked the lantern from her saddle, extending it to the older woman. "Then you had best carry the light, then."

Meradyth took the lantern with a resolute nod.

The pair did not hesitate—they thundered through the shadowy tunnels, going as fast as the lynxes' powerful paws could carry them. They crashed through wispy webs, then caught up to Blazeclaw in a pitch-black cavern where the shadows dripped as thick as ink.

In the darkness, Faerin didn't see the warriors on their flanks.

A nerubian slammed into her, sending her sprawling across the web-strewn ground. Her hireling lynx hit the floor beside her, hissing. To her great surprise, the big cat didn't turn tail and run; instead, it leaped to its feet and pounced on the nerubian, knocking it down with a snarl. Blazeclaw screamed, pouncing on the creature and sinking her fangs into its throat.

A second nerubian warrior lunged at the lynxes, ready to drive a pincer into Blazeclaw's broad back.

With a shout, Faerin charged at the second nerubian, tearing her javelin from its sheath on her back. She turned the point of her weapon upward and drove it through the creature's unprotected chin. The tip of her javelin burst through the top of the warrior's skull. Still more of them swarmed from the darkness, their eyes dancing like wicked stars. Six, no, eight—too many to count.

As the nerubian slumped in front of Faerin, dead, another big cat bounded into the fray with a rider on its back: Meradyth. Her sword glinted as she and Stoutheart dove between two new enemies, and she held Faerin's lantern high. The imperial lynx tore a foreleg from a socket. Meradyth blocked a bite with her blade, then sliced off the spider's jaw.

LITTLE SPARK

The battle was brutal, outnumbered as they were. The lantern's light sputtered but did not die. They fought until the webs underfoot grew spongy with black blood, until the eyes began to wink out around them, until the nerubians began to skitter back.

In her carelessness, one warrior landed a blow on Faerin's left side, throwing her to the ground. Something loosened in her chest, sending a sharp pain down her spine. The warrior lifted one massive leg to gut her—wincing, she rolled out of its range. Faerin grabbed her javelin and pushed back to her feet.

The warrior gave her no chance to recover. It charged forward, slashing at her torso. Faerin's hireling lynx pounced onto the creature, knocking the warrior off balance. Faerin plunged her javelin into battle-churned gravel. Light crackled through the ground, consecrating it against the shadows. The warrior shrieked and staggered back, giving her time to tap into the Sacred Flame and shoot forth a blade of brilliant, burning Holy Light. The Light slammed into the warrior's chest, cracking the exoskeleton and leaving its innards exposed. With a high-pitched scream, the great cat gutted the nerubian.

As Faerin ripped her javelin free, shouts echoed through the corridors. Andryck swept to her side, while Eoghan protected her left flank with his shield. The nerubians fled at the sight of reinforcements, leaving their dead behind.

"Why have you
come so deep into these
caverns? This a dangerous
gambit, even for you."

"Blazeclaw led us here," Faerin said, nodding
to the great cat. "Ryton and the others can't
be far—we may save them yet if we hurry."

"Flame preserve us," Andryck said,
but he made no move
to stop her.

LITTLE SPARK

"Faerin!" Andryck said, holding his lantern high as he scanned her for injuries. He gripped her shoulder with his free hand, giving her a little shake. "Are you all right?"

"I'm fine," she replied. "How did you find us so quickly?"

"The screaming was a fair indication," he replied with a grin, but it died away quickly. "Why have you come so deep into these caverns? This a dangerous gambit, even for you."

"Blazeclaw led us here," Faerin said, nodding to the great cat. "Ryton and the others can't be far—we may save them yet if we hurry."

"Flame preserve us," Andryck said, but he made no move to stop her. Faerin took point with Blazeclaw, while Eoghan brought up the rear. No one spoke—they communicated in hand gestures, moving as silently as possible. Andryck walked to Faerin's left side, bearing a lantern in one hand, his sword in the other. Meradyth followed them, clutching Faerin's lantern close. The cats made no sound, padding on soft paws.

They followed the nerubians' trail deeper into the caves, winding their way through abandoned tunnels. Webs draped from the ceilings like funeral shrouds. The stuff stuck to Faerin's boots and trailed off her armor. Pinpricks of light danced down the corridors, the silence heavy enough to suffocate.

The farther they ventured, the more anxious Faerin became. Even if they managed to locate the abducted Arathi, what was to say they would be able to escape this warren? Faerin had lost track of the path ten turns ago, and though she trusted the lynxes to find the trail again, swarms of nerubians could find them *first*.

In another hundred yards, a muffled scream echoed through the tunnels. Faerin paused, gesturing to the others. Meradyth lifted her lantern and tilted her head, listening.

When a second scream reached their ears, Faerin hurried in its direction. She and her comrades emerged in a massive, lightless cavern, one with a floor crisscrossed with webs and littered with carcasses. Clutches of egg sacs pulsated in dark corners. The place smelled like a mixture of rot and excrement— the odor made Faerin's eyes water. She nudged a dented helm with her foot, recoiling when she recognized its shape. Ryton had forged that helm, and her javelin had put the nick in its left temple not a fortnight ago.

No, Ryton. Her next breath was half a shudder, half a sob. *You are truly gone, then.*

Andryck joined her, holding his lantern high. "Look there," he murmured, pointing into the shadows. On the very edge of the light, human-shaped figures writhed within tight cocoons of spider's silk. Faerin gripped her javelin, relieved to see the villagers still lived. Had the nerubians left their prey unguarded? It didn't seem possible. Faerin stepped deeper into the room, scanning the shadows for movement.

Behind her, one of the lynxes growled.

Glittering eyes opened in the darkness. Faerin gave a shout as a hulking nerubian beast emerged from a darkened corner, the like of which she had never seen. It stood three times as tall as a warrior, looming over Faerin and the others, chittering, snarling. Answering calls barreled through the adjoining corridors, followed by a swarm of nerubian warriors at least two dozen strong.

The gigantic creature did not hesitate. It crashed into Meradyth and Stoutheart with ferocious might, knocking Faerin's lantern from the woman's hand. The flames scattered as they hit the ground, sending up a shower of sparks. As the light winked out, a thick, impenetrable wall of darkness fell around her.

Meradyth screamed—whether in agony, in fear, or some twisted combination of the two, Faerin could not tell. Stoutheart loosed a roar, making the whole cavern tremble with the sound of his voice.

"Meradyth!" Faerin called, but before she could go to the woman's aid, the nerubian warriors fell upon them.

On instinct, Faerin consecrated the ground below her feet, giving the barest amount of Light to fight by. Her lynx prowled past her like a shadow, leaping on the closest nerubian with a shriek. While her eye adjusted, another nerubian feinted right but struck left, slamming one of its legs into Faerin's rib cage. A sharp pain stabbed into her side again, bright sparks across her vision. She gasped, staggering, but did not fall. The pain made her breath run ragged—she would not survive a third such blow.

Dodging the warrior's next attack, Faerin concentrated the Sacred Flame in her fist and shot forth dazzling Light, blinding every nerubian within ten yards of her position. As the shadows rushed back, she could just make out Meradyth's shivering, shaking form on the floor. Stoutheart battled the massive nerubian back, protecting his rider.

She could just barely hear Meradyth's sobs.

"Meradyth," Faerin nearly screamed, voice raw. "You must rally, or else we shall be overrun!"

"Go to her, Faerin," Andryck shouted, blocking an attack with his shield. "I will distract the behemoth."

Andryck could not hope to hold such a gargantuan beast at bay, not while surrounded by so many warriors. Before she could protest, Andryck shouted, "Go!"

The word spurred Faerin forward. She sprinted across the room as Andryck taunted the great beast away from Meradyth and her lynx. The creature smashed through its fellows to reach the paladin. Faerin scrambled past their enemies, then fell on her knees beside Meradyth.

LITTLE SPARK

"You have to get up," Faerin said, putting her javelin down to shake the other woman by the shoulder. "We must fight together if we are to survive!"

"I can't," Meradyth howled. "I-I'm sorry, I'm not like you— the Flame has forsaken me!"

"That isn't true, Meradyth," Faerin shouted, pleading. "You must have faith!"

The nerubians shook off the stun. Faerin could hear more of them scrabbling down the halls, and the floor trembled under their steps. To their left, Andryck and Eoghan battled the hulking beast, their lynxes barely keeping its warriors at bay. Blood gushed from a grievous wound on Eoghan's arm. Andryck staggered under another attack.

The two men would not hold much longer. Not alone.

In a moment of inspiration—or perhaps desperation—Faerin grabbed Meradyth's hand. She felt the spark of the Sacred Flame there, dim as it was in the woman. "A spark still burns within you, Meradyth," she said. "Think not on your fears, but of whom you fight for!"

With those words, Faerin pushed the battle and encroaching darkness far from her mind. She summoned her every memory of Ryton Blackholme: Every extra tart he filched for her, every hand up he'd given her during training, every brotherly embrace, every cheeky grin . . . until she felt the Sacred Flame blaze bright inside her heart. It burned away those long, dark hours she spent trapped in the airship's hull; the endless days and nights of Steelstrike's orders; the fears she held of her perceived inadequacies, the insults, the unbearable *pity* from others—everything burned away in that moment, leaving only brilliance.

A Beacon of Light burst from Faerin's fingertips, cutting through the darkness and gilding Meradyth's head and shoulders with its glow. "Rise, children of the Arathi!" Faerin's voice rang through the cavern like a bell. "We shall not give in to darkness and despair this day!"

Grabbing her javelin off the ground, Faerin rose to the oncoming shadows. One of the nerubian warriors leaped at her, while another circled to attack her left flank. She sidestepped the first, slashing one of its delicate leg joints. A spray of fluid burst from the joint. Faerin spun to avoid getting soaked. The beast screeched, its foreleg collapsing.

A shadow twitched, and a second warrior dove at her. She parried its attack with her javelin, grunting. The nerubian curled its claws around her javelin's shaft, drawing her close, venom dripping from its mandibles.

Releasing her javelin, she stunned the nerubian with a blazing blessed hammer made from Holy Light. When the warrior dropped her blade, Faerin snatched it from the air, swung it around, and slashed the creature's throat open. The

She summoned
her every memory of Ryton
Blackholme: Every extra tart he
filched for her, every hand up he'd given her
during training, every brotherly embrace, every
cheeky grin . . . until she felt the Sacred Flame
blaze bright inside her heart. It burned away those
long, dark hours she spent trapped in the airship's
hull; the endless days and nights of Steelstrike's
orders; the fears she held of her perceived
inadequacies, the insults, the unbearable
pity from others—everything burned
away in that moment, leaving
only brilliance.

creature staggered, trying to press its claws into the wound, then collapsed.

Faerin felt the tremors in the ground beneath her a breath too late. She pivoted, realizing that another nerubian warrior charged from her unprotected left side. Her heart seized. Faerin barely heard Meradyth's warning shout; the moments stretched longer, and time slowed. Faerin had no time to correct her stance, to set up a counterattack, or even to parry—the warrior would reach her in the next blink.

A bright light—fierce as Faerin's memory of the noonday sun—sliced through the nerubian at the pedicle, burning the creature to ash. Faerin whirled, surprised to see Meradyth standing not ten paces away, her hands aglow with the Sacred Flame.

Meradyth blinked at Faerin in surprise.

"We burn brighter together, Meradyth Lacke," Faerin hollered. Her voice stayed steady and true—it did not betray her in that moment, even as fear and adrenaline made her blood run hot. "Come, let us teach the nerubians to fear the Sacred Flame!"

A host of nerubians dropped from the ceiling. As the swarm skittered toward them, chittering loudly, Faerin summoned a blessed hammer over the hulking swarm leader, then dropped it onto the creature's head. It hit home, ringing out like a bell. The nerubian reeled, its legs spasming, and crashed to the ground.

In the dim light, the lynxes charged forward, a rage of claws and teeth. Meradyth fought at Faerin's side, sending bright bolts of the Sacred Flame into the swarm. The warriors came next—Faerin consecrated the ground underfoot, then jammed her javelin into one of the creature's exposed chests. Light-filled cracks raced through the nerubian's carapace. The beast shrieked and reared back, yanking the javelin from Faerin's grip.

The battle took minutes; the battle took an age. Faerin's heart was beating so wildly, it was hard to track the passage of time. Before long, the nerubians sounded a retreat, shrinking into the shadows. When they were gone, Faerin and Meradyth cut free the villagers of Beledar's Bounty. Ryton was not among them. Faerin retrieved his helm from the darkness, only to find it slicked with dried blood. When Blazeclaw pawed at it, Faerin tied the helm to her saddle.

Faerin would mourn the loss of Ryton, but she would celebrate the salvation of her people.

"You braved the darkness . . . for *us*?" one man asked, confused. "Against the general's orders?"

"The Sacred Flame burns brightest in the darkness," Meradyth said, taking one of the children by the hand.

Faerin smiled, for Meradyth's fingertips still burned with Holy Light.

"You braved the
darkness . . . for *us*?" one man
asked, confused. "Against the
general's orders?"

"The Sacred Flame burns brightest in the
darkness," Meradyth said, taking one of
the children by the hand.

Faerin smiled, for Meradyth's
fingertips still burned with
Holy Light.

LITTLE SPARK

It took three days for Beledar's light to return, and when it did, General Steelstrike relieved Faerin of her duties to the Arathi army, citing her egregious breach of protocol.

Faerin hadn't expected anything less.

As she ascended one of Mereldar's many hills, Steelstrike's words played in her head:

Though I am grateful you managed to save the people of Beledar's Bounty, your actions were extremely reckless. Foolish. You are one of the most talented paladins and fighters I have ever seen, Faerin, but it's become clear you do not possess an officer's temperament.

Faerin's lips had twitched into a half grin, goading Steelstrike into a frown. *I couldn't agree more, General. I am not fit for the service,* Faerin had replied. *But to be quite honest, I learned such recklessness from you.*

Steelstrike's eyes widened to the size of saucers. The woman stood a little straighter, drawing her shoulders back and slitting her eyes. *You had best choose your next words carefully, Faerin, for you have already spent the remainder of my patience today.*

Did you not venture into the darkness to save me, General? Faerin had replied. *Did you not carry the Sacred Flame into the shadows on my behalf? Can you not see the strength of the Flame you kindled within me that day?*

Steelstrike had opened her mouth to speak, but Faerin hurried on, unable to face more of the general's condemnation while bearing her heart so wholly. *By saving my life, you forged a deep desire in me to help others. Try as I might, I can't seem to break myself of it—and for that . . . I will always be grateful to you.*

Before the general could respond, Faerin had turned on her heel and fled the room. She hadn't thought about how that exchange would go beyond her breathless declaration, so she retreated. Quickly, and before Steelstrike could call her back.

Even if Steelstrike hadn't dismissed her, Faerin knew she would never have found happiness among the army's ranks. Still . . . it had given her a purpose. No, a place.

She plucked a small flower from the grass around her, twirling it between her fingers, sitting with an unfamiliar sense of despair. What *would* she do now? Become a farmer and scratch food from Hallowfall's rocky soil? Pick up a hammer a learn the smith's art? Or perhaps she could make her way by protecting the people Steelstrike couldn't or wouldn't—but she wasn't sure she wanted so lonely a life.

Behind her, footsteps vibrated through the soil. Faerin sighed. The only person who had ever disturbed her here was Ryton, and he was gone; Steelstrike must have followed her from the keep. "With all due respect, General, I don't want to talk about it," she said, her voice tinged with annoyance. She tossed the little flower aside. "I need some time to think."

"The general is a hard woman," a gruff, unrecognizable voice said. "But her unyielding will has seen our people through the darkest of times."

Faerin's eyes widened. She leaped to her feet and turned, shocked to find the Great Kyron standing behind her. Andari, one of his best Lamplighters, stood with them . . . as did *Meradyth*.

Faerin drew a sharp breath of surprise. How often had she observed and admired the Great Kyron and Andari from afar? Their names had already been inscribed in history, and someday, they would pass into legend.

Kyron squinted up at Beledar's light. "Meradyth told me a most interesting story about your experiences in Beledar's Bounty," they said, shifting their gaze back to Faerin. "She says that you were the spark that kindled the Sacred Flame within her. Now that you are released from Steelstrike's ranks, she would like to recommend you to ours."

Faerin sputtered, looking at Meradyth askance. "Really?" was all she could manage to say, for she thought her tongue might have turned to lead.

Meradyth folded her hands in front of her. Her brows furrowed, deepening the persistent worry lines in her forehead. "I've chosen to leave my position at the Priory as well."

"*What?* Why would you do such a thing?" Faerin asked, stepping forward, her heart in a twist. "Your faith *defines* you."

"It isn't so much that my faith is shaken," Meradyth continued. "On the contrary, it's completely *renewed*. While I remain dedicated to the empire—and, by extension, the Sacred Flame—I've realized that my prayers in the Priory will not deliver our people. I, too, will need to take up arms in their defense—as you taught me in the depths."

Meradyth paused, took a deep breath, then bobbed her head, almost as if she was still trying to convince herself of the rightness of her actions. "I informed General Steelstrike today that I intend to leave the reserves. I'd like to train as a Lamplighter, and I think . . . you should too, Faerin."

"General Steelstrike will never allow it," Faerin said, looking to Kyron. "She has refused me before."

"Aye, she wanted very much to count you among her ranks," Kyron replied. "But she understands that some flames are not fit for hearths and forges—some are made for the dawntowers, pushing back against the endless night."

"You taught me to have a faith greater than my fears," Meradyth said, clasping her hands in front of her and performing a bow. "No one deserves this more than you, Faerin."

Faerin lifted her chin and swallowed hard, hoping the others didn't notice the way her cheeks colored with embarrassment.

Kyron continued, "Should you wish to join the Lamplighters, Faerin Lothar, we would welcome you."

"It's all I've ever wanted," Faerin said, surprised by the emotion in her voice. She locked eyes with Andari, who winked.

"Come, then," Kyron said with a smile. "Let us talk."

ABOUT THE AUTHORS

JONATHAN MABERRY is a *New York Times* bestselling author, five-time Bram Stoker Award winner, four-time Scribe Award winner, Inkpot Award winner, comic book writer, executive producer, and writing teacher. He is the author of fifty novels, 160 short stories, twenty-two graphic novels, and twenty nonfiction books, and he has edited twenty-five anthologies. His vampire apocalypse book series V-Wars was a Netflix original series. He writes horror, science fiction, epic fantasy, mystery, adventure, thrillers, and more. He is the president of the International Association of Media Tie-In Writers and the editor of *Weird Tales* magazine. Find him at www.jonathanmaberry. com and everywhere on social media.

CHRISTIE GOLDEN, award-winning *New York Times* bestselling author, has worked with Blizzard Entertainment for nearly a quarter of a century. She's written more than sixty books, including *Arthas: Rise of the Lich King* and *Sylvanas*. Audiobook fans can hear Christie narrate some of her Blizzard titles on Audible. During her years as a formal employee, Golden authored *World of Warcraft* cinematics and cutscenes, *Hearthstone* song lyrics, as well as short stories and other projects for *Overwatch* and *Diablo*.

DELILAH S. DAWSON is the author of the *New York Times* bestseller *Star Wars: Phasma*, as well as *Star Wars Inquisitor: Rise of the Red Blade*, *Star Wars: Galaxy's Edge: Black Spire*, *The Violence*, *Bloom*, *Mine*, *Camp Scare*, the Hit series, the Blud series, and the creator-owned comics *Ladycastle*, *Sparrowhawk*, and *Star Pig*, and the Shadow series (written as Lila Bowen). With Kevin Hearne, she cowrites the Tales of Pell. She lives in Georgia with her family.

CATHERYNNE M. VALENTE is the *New York Times* bestselling author of over forty works of fiction and poetry, including *Space Opera*, *Palimpsest*, *Deathless*, *Radiance*, *Mass Effect: Annihilation*, and the crowdfunded phenomenon *The Girl Who Circumnavigated Fairyland in a Ship of Her Own Making*. She is the winner of the Nebula, Hugo, Otherwise, Sturgeon, Mythopoeic, Lambda, and Locus Awards, among others. She lives on an island off the coast of Maine with her son.

ANDREW ROBINSON is a prolific animation writer and creator who has worked for companies like Marvel, WB, Hasbro, Cartoon Network, Sony, and others on IP like Transformers, Spider-Man, Avengers, Young Justice, G.I. Joe, and more. Since joining Blizzard Entertainment in 2014, he has written animated shorts, songs, world-building lore, comics, and short stories for all their games, and is eager to bring Blizzard's fans more.

COURTNEY ALAMEDA is a novelist and lifelong gamer. After almost fifteen years of writing professionally, Courtney has worked in a broad spectrum of genres and industries, though horror still has her heart. Born and raised in the San Francisco Bay area, she now resides in the northwestern United States with her husband, one dog, two cats, three library rooms, and whatever monsters lurk in the rural darkness around her home.

WRITTEN BY
Jonathan Maberry, Christie Golden, Delilah S. Dawson,
Catherynne M. Valente, Andrew Robinson, Courtney Alameda

EDITED BY
Chloe Fraboni, Eric Geron

ILLUSTRATED BY
Ognjen Sporin

ART DIRECTION BY
Corey Peterschmidt

DESIGNED BY
Jessica Rodriguez

PRODUCED BY
Brianne Messina, Amber Proue-Thibodeau

LORE CONSULTATION BY
Courtney Chavez, Sean Copeland

GAME TEAM CONSULTATION BY
Steve Aguilar, Raphael Ahad, Ely Cannon, Steve Danuser,
Mark Kaleda, Nicholas McDowell, Chris Metzen,
Justin Parker, Stacey Phillips, Korey Regan, Stephanie Yoon

BLIZZARD ENTERTAINMENT

Manager, Publishing: **PETER MOLINARI**
Associate Manager, Consumer Products: **CHANEE' GOUDE**
Senior Director, Story & Franchise Development: **VENECIA DURAN**
Senior Manager, Writing & Books: **MATTHEW COHAN**
Senior Producer, Books: **BRIANNE MESSINA**
Associate Producer, Books: **AMBER PROUE-THIBODEAU**
Editorial Supervisor: **CHLOE FRABONI**
Senior Brand Artist: **COREY PETERSCHMIDT**
Associate Manager, Creative Development Production: **JAMIE ORTIZ**
Producer, Lore: **ED FOX**
Lore Historian Lead: **SEAN COPELAND**
Associate Historian: **IAN LANDA-BEAVERS**